THE BIG BOOK OF DRAWING

Woo! jr
kiDS aCtivities

Woo! Jr. Kids Activities Founder: Wendy Piersall

Book Layout by: Lilia Garvin
Cover Illustration: Michael Koch

Published by DragonFruit, an imprint of Mango Publishing, a division of Mango Publishing Group, Inc.

For permission requests, please contact the publisher at:

Mango Publishing Group
2850 Douglas Road, 2nd Floor
Coral Gables, FL 33134 USA
info@mango.bz

For special orders, quantity sales, course adoptions and corporate sales, please email the publisher at sales@mango.bz. For trade and wholesale sales, please contact Ingram Publisher Services at customer.service@ingramcontent.com or +1.800.509.4887.

The Big Book of Drawing

ISBN: (p) 978-1-64250-672-3

TABLE OF CONTENTS

All you need is a pencil, eraser, and a piece of paper!

Follow each drawing diagram step by step:

TiPS & TRiCKS

Draw lightly at first, because you might need to erase some lines as you work.

Add details according to the diagrams, but don't worry about being perfect! Artists frequently make mistakes - they just find ways to make their mistakes look interesting. You can erase mistakes, or use them as a new decoration.

Don't worry if your drawings don't turn out quite the way you want them to. Just keep practicing! Sometimes drawing the same thing just a few times will help.

You can draw a new animal or object every day, or several each day. For an extra challenge, use your creativity to combine multiple drawings into an entire scene, like the one below.

OUTER SPACE SCENE

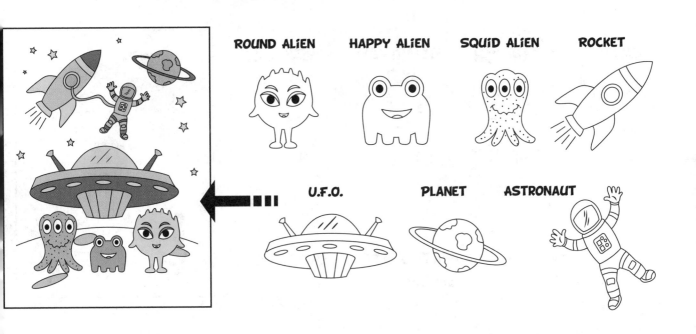

ROUND ALIEN

HAPPY ALIEN

SQUID ALIEN

ROCKET

U.F.O.

PLANET

ASTRONAUT

Turn the page for more cool composition ideas!

CREATE MORE FULL SCENES

Check out these scenes.

In the Underwater Scene example, a mermaid swims with other sea creatures. You can find the Mermaid in the Scifi & Fantasy section of this book, and the other animals are in the Water Animals section.

When you create your own scenes, remember you can take drawings from different sections to make unique scenes.

- UNDERWATER SCENE -

CRAB

ROYAL STARFISH

STINGRAY

MERMAID

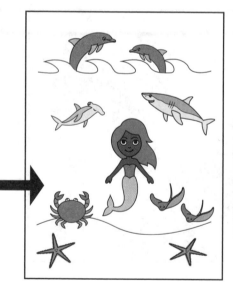

HAMMERHEAD SHARK

GREAT WHITE SHARK

DOLPHIN

- FLYING FAIRIES SCENE -

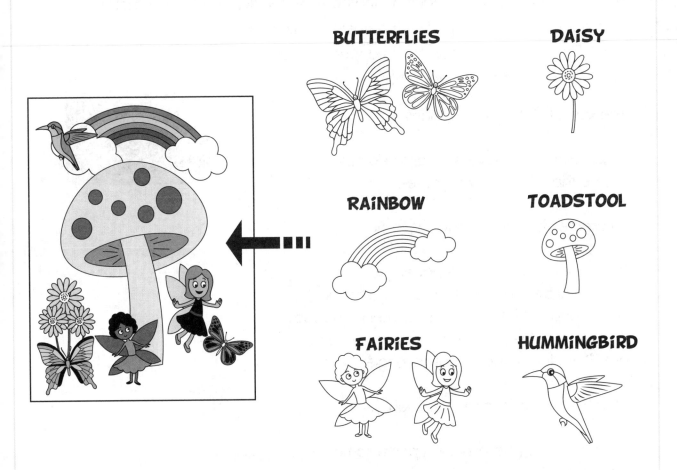

BUTTERFLIES

DAISY

RAINBOW

TOADSTOOL

FAIRIES

HUMMINGBIRD

There is no limit to the type of scenes you can draw when you use your imagination! You can take your favorite step-by-step tutorials and decorate them on a page, even at different sizes, like above. When the toadstool in the Flying Fairies Scene is big, it makes the fairies and butterflies look small!

Play around with sizes, and create your own scenes!

ADD PERSPECTIVE TO YOUR DRAWINGS BY USING THE VANISHING POINT AND A PERSPECTIVE GRID!

The "vanishing point" is a point on the horizon in which a set of parallel lines appear to converge (join together) into a single point. For example, railroad tracks appear to converge in the distance in this photograph:

The key is DRAWING with lines.

One point perspecive is a centered place where the viewer's eye focuses.

To create your own, follow these steps:

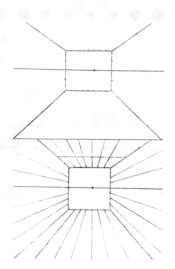

1) Near the center of the paper, place your ruler to draw a horizontal line in the middle of the paper. Make sure it is parallel to the top & bottom of the page, meaning your ruler is even with them and isn't at an angle.

2) Draw the horizon line very lightly.

3) Place a dot (the vanishing point) somewhere on that line.

4) Draw very light pressure lines radiating and converging (meeting) toward the vanishing point.

Congratulations! You've now drawn a One Point Perspective Grid.

TWO-POINT PERSPECTIVE

1. Near the center of the paper PLAN and place your ruler to draw a horizontal line parallel to the top and bottom of the paper. Draw that Horizon Line very lightly.

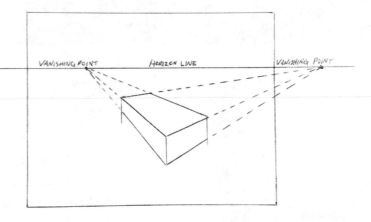

2. Place TWO dots (vanishing points) somewhere on that line. The two points must be on the line but can be outside of the sides of the picture area, such as the vanishing point on the right in the example above.

3. Draw very light pressure lines radiating and converging to the vanishing point. You are now ready to draw objects onto that illusion of 3 dimensional space. If the objects are buildings, then all of the details of the structure are drawn along the dotted grid lines you've created with your Two Point Perspective Grid.

4. Draw the tops and bottoms of every detail so that those lines recede (or go back) in space to the Vanishing Point.

5. Again, all of the vertical lines in the picture must be parallel to the right and left sides of your paper. An example of two point perspective drawing can be seen in Vincent Van Gogh's The Yellow House:

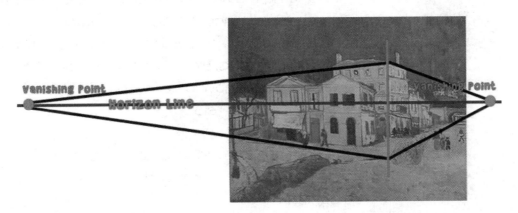

WANT TO ADD MORE DETAIL?

You can introduce shading techniques to make your drawings even more realistic and fun! Once you have finished your lines, consider shading in one of these ways:

SHADING TECHNIQUE: HATCHING

In hatching, draw lots of lines that don't cross. You can press harder with your pencil to make darker lines, and space them closer together for a more full, consistent gradient (in art, a gradient is a transition from one color or shade to another.)

Anywhere you put marks on the paper it will look darker. For your lightest spots, don't put any marks.

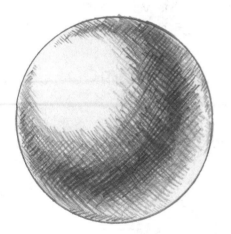

SHADING TECHNIQUE: CROSS-HATCHING

Cross-hatching is very similar to hatching. The key difference is that you now also want to make marks coming from a second direction. Practice this technique with pencil or pen. They're both very good materials to cross-hatch with!

SHADING TECHNIQUE: SCUMBLING

Scumbling is a method where you shade with much more random marks than hatching, or cross-hatching. To scumble, use circular and squiggling marks. Don't worry what direction your pencil is moving in. Try to keep your wrist loose, and relax.

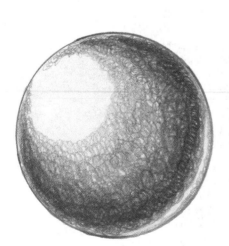

Remember to overlap, or layer, your marks, and put them closer together in your darkest areas.

SHADING TECHNIQUE: STIPPLING

Stippling is also known as pointillism. To stipple, you shade with many, many small dots. This is a bit similar to how pixels are used to shade on a computer screen.

The closeness, or density, of your dots will determine your darkest points. Choose a starting point, and then carefully lift your pencil or pen up, and press down to make your dots. Try to avoid making any lines, or marks.

SHADING TECHNIQUE: BLENDING

With blending, the marks you make on the paper don't matter as much. You can start with hatched, cross-hatched, or scumbled marks. Try to make your shading smooth, and close together.

Next, rub the pencil marks together. You can use a facial tissue, napkin, or even your fingers. Afterward, make sure to clean your hands when you're done. It's messy!

EXAMPLE

PRACTICING VALUE

In art, value means the degree of lightness or darkness of a color. Right now, since we're shading with pencil, that color is black, and the variation in value is called a grayscale. We're going to practice making them.

Use the scale to shade from light to dark. The paper can be your lightest shade. Press a bit harder for each new shade, until you get to the darkest.

YOU CAN PRACTICE HERE

...AND HERE!

If you want to practice more, you can! First, draw a line of squares. Use a ruler to help you, or any hard surface. It's okay if the lines aren't perfect - then shade!

TIPS & REMINDERS

Varying shading on large areas can add texture to your favorite animals.

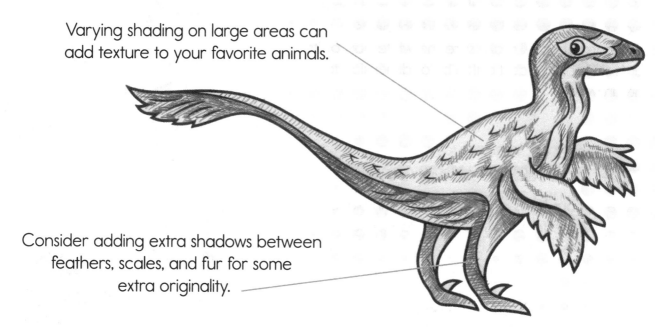

Consider adding extra shadows between feathers, scales, and fur for some extra originality.

Try it yourself!
You can find the Deinonychus on page 178.

You can ink your lines and erase the pencil marks beneath before shading.

Leave the paper blank, or use an eraser for highlights.

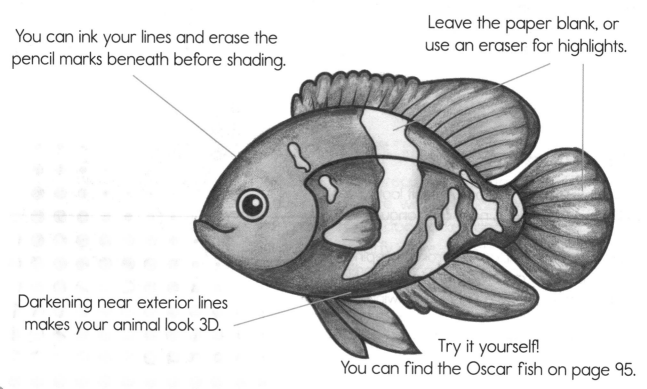

Darkening near exterior lines makes your animal look 3D.

Try it yourself!
You can find the Oscar fish on page 95.

ADDING COLOR!

Another way to decorate your drawings and scenes is to add color. Did you know that there are different colors known as primary colors, secondary colors, and tertiary colors? Let's check them out!

PRIMARY COLORS

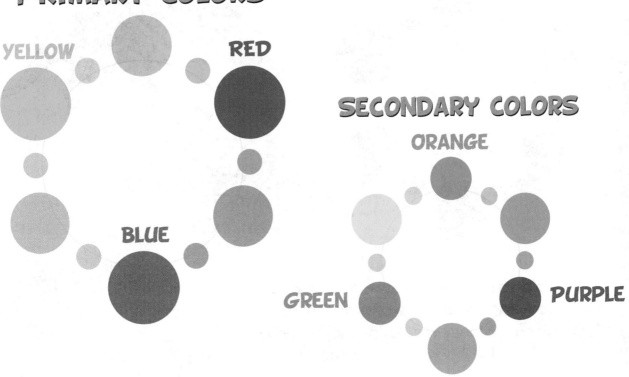

YELLOW

RED

BLUE

SECONDARY COLORS

ORANGE

GREEN

PURPLE

TERTIARY COLORS

Yellow-Orange

Red-Orange

Yellow-Orange

Red-Purple

Blue-Green

Blue-Purple

COMPLEMENTARY COLORS

One simple way to find colors that look very good together is to draw a line straight across the color wheel. Let's take a look!

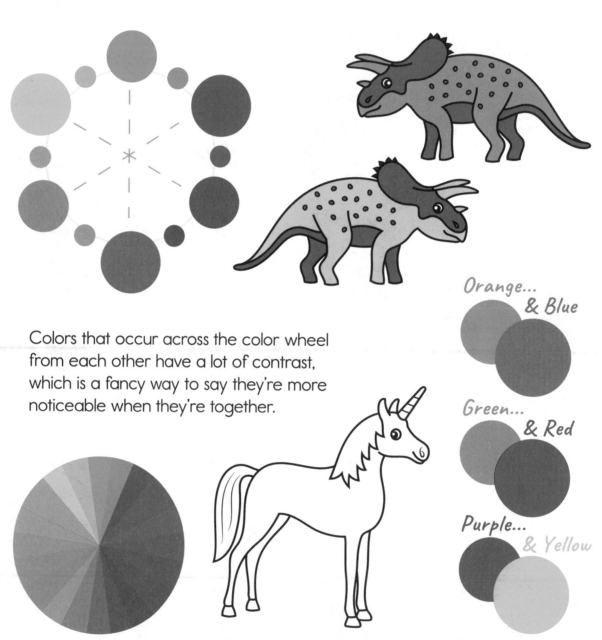

Colors that occur across the color wheel from each other have a lot of contrast, which is a fancy way to say they're more noticeable when they're together.

Orange...
& Blue

Green...
& Red

Purple...
& Yellow

PICK YOUR FAVORITE COMPLEMENTARY COLORS & COLOR THE UNICORN!

Analagous colors are a special way of picking colors by only choosing colors next to each other. So, one group of adjacent analagous colors are orange, orange-red, and red. Another are green, light-green, and yellow.

To explore analagous colors, let's try blending from one color to another! First we'll go from orange to red, then purple to blue, and finally yellow to green.

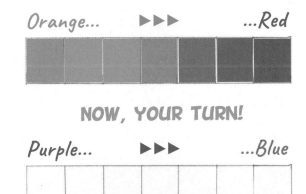

Orange... ▶▶▶ ...Red

NOW, YOUR TURN!

Purple... ▶▶▶ ...Blue

Yellow... ▶▶▶ ...Green

TASTY TREATS

Lemon

Strawberry

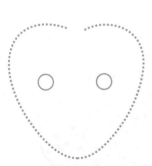   

Pear

Pancakes

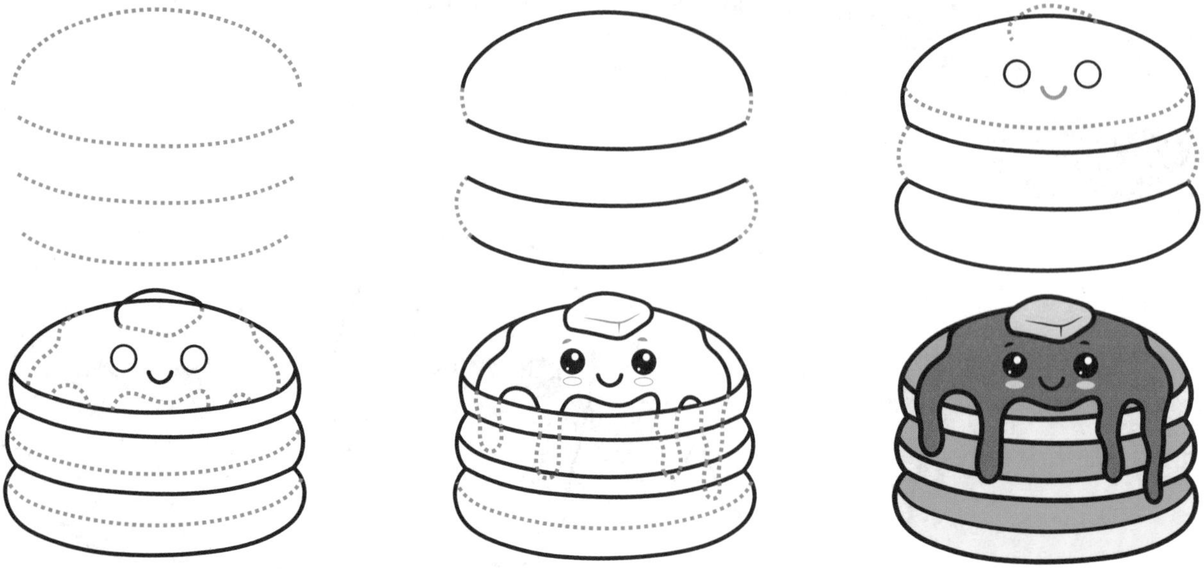

Donut

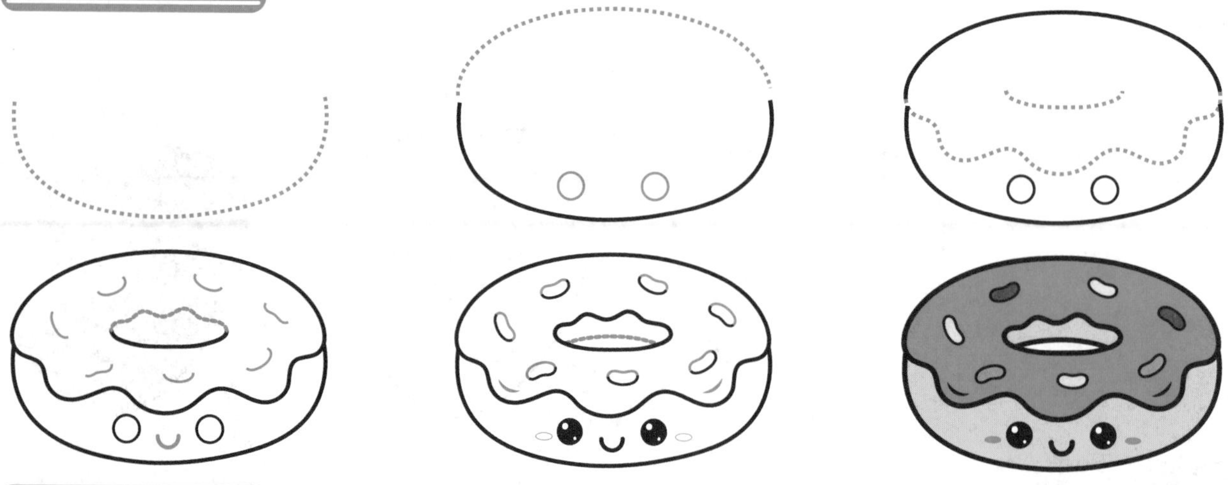

Pizza

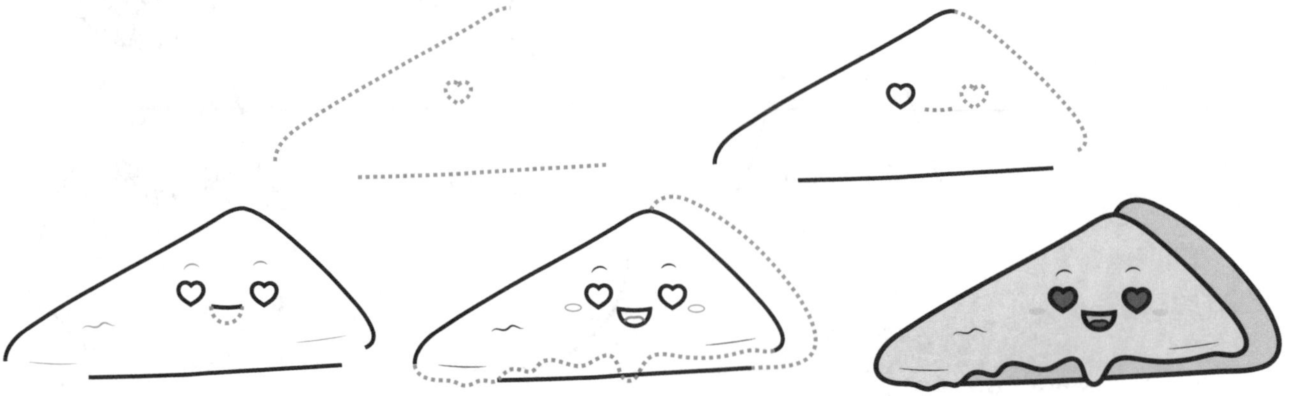

Pretzel

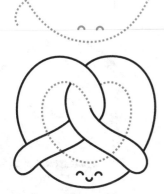
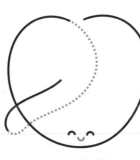
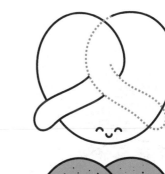

Cheese

Croissant

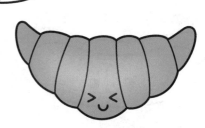

Toast

Egg

Hotdog

Dumpling

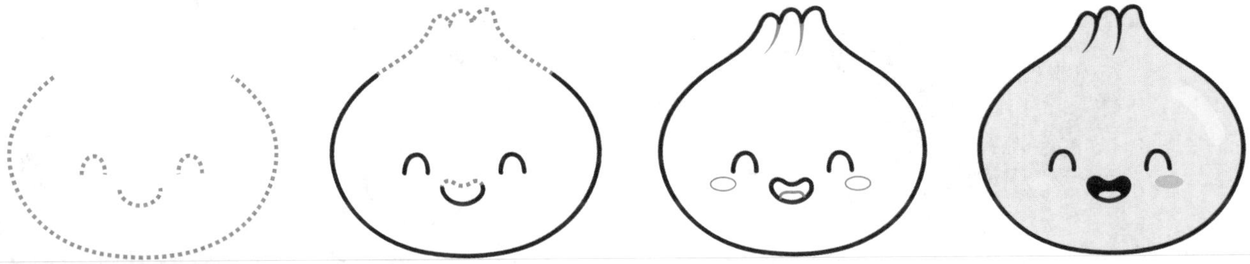

Taco

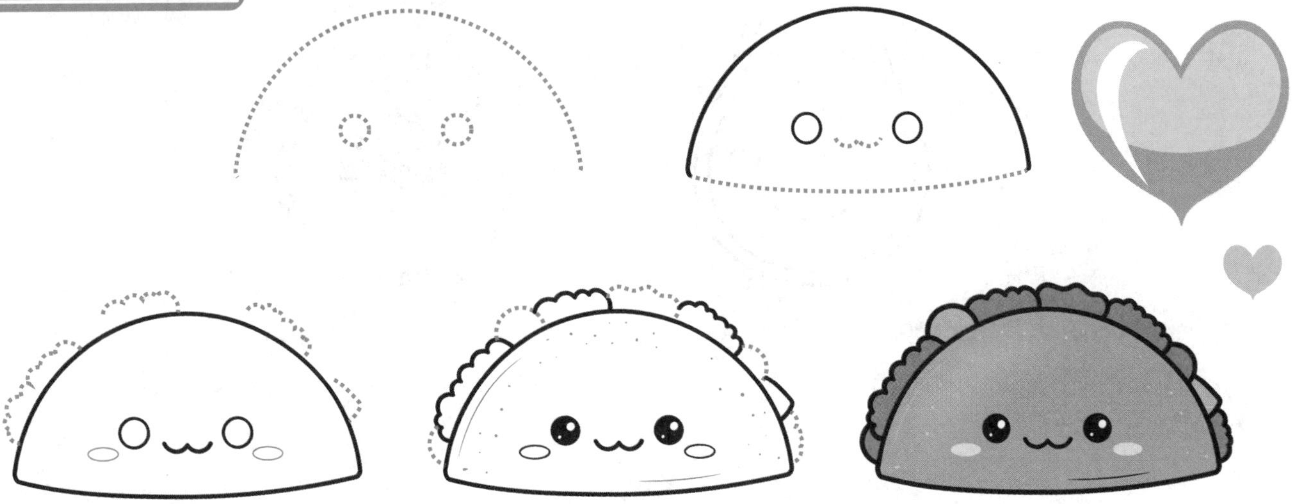

Sushi

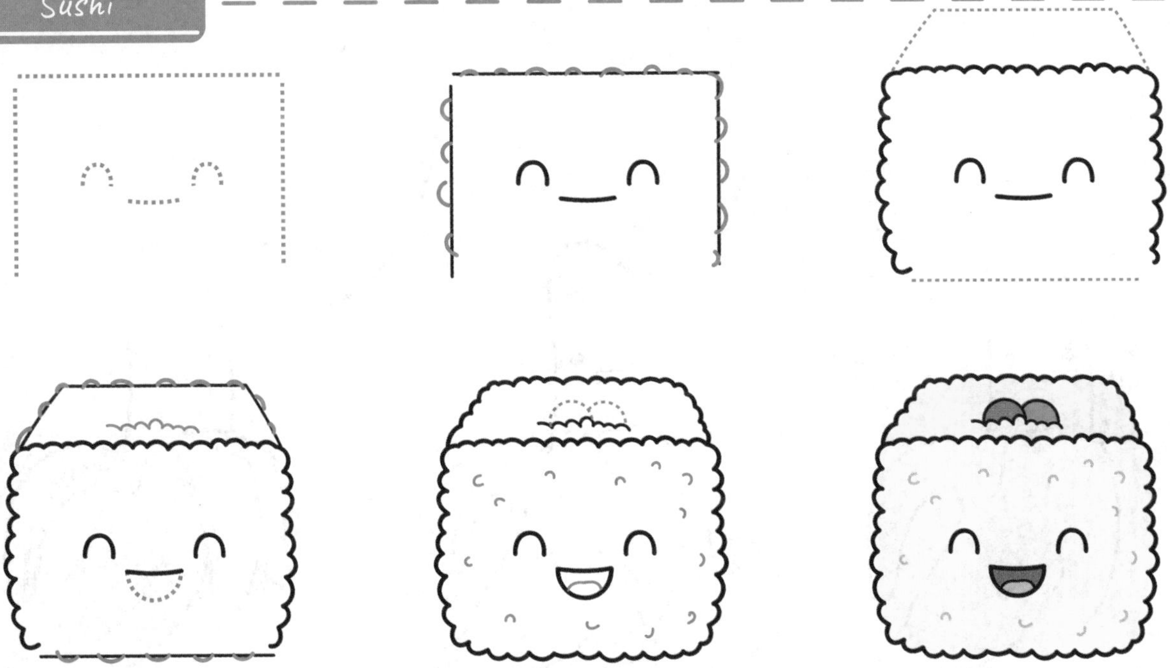

Avocado

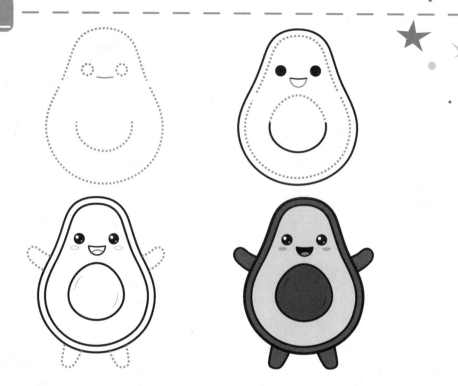

Banana

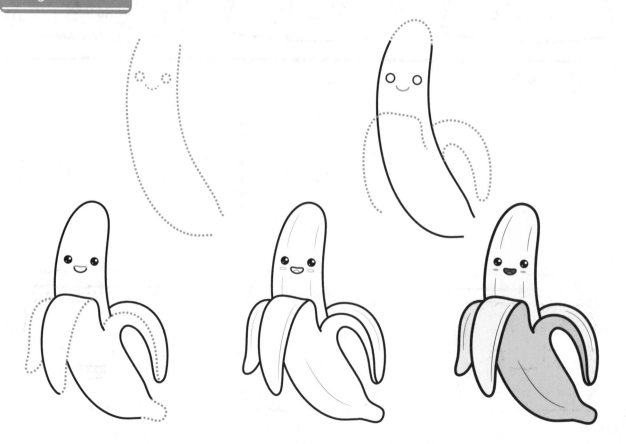

Raspberry

Coconut

Green Pepper

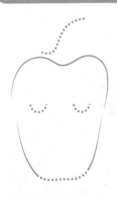 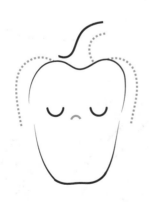 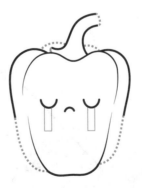 

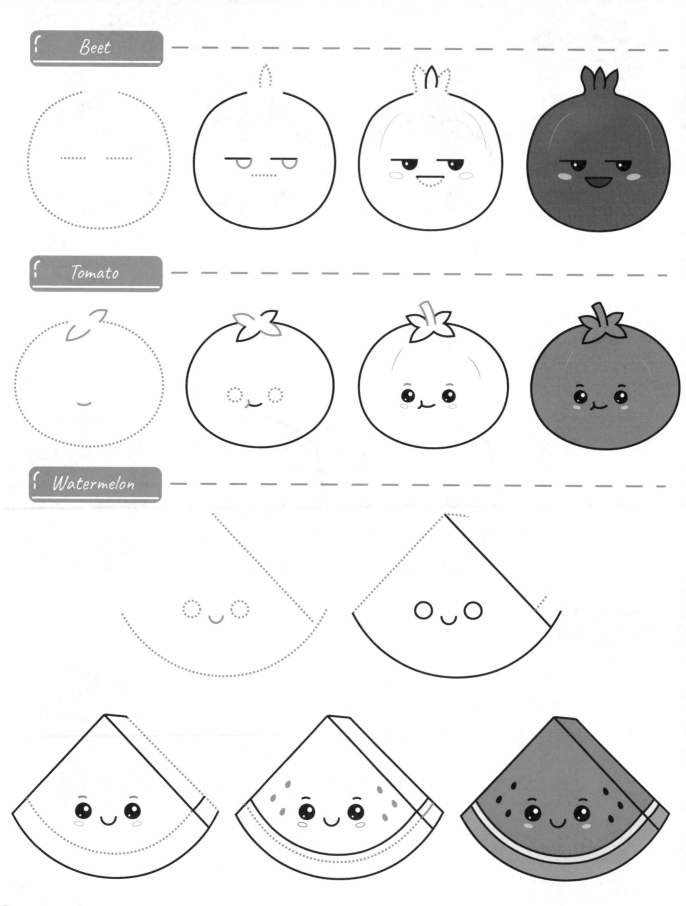

Honey

Cookie

Flan Cake

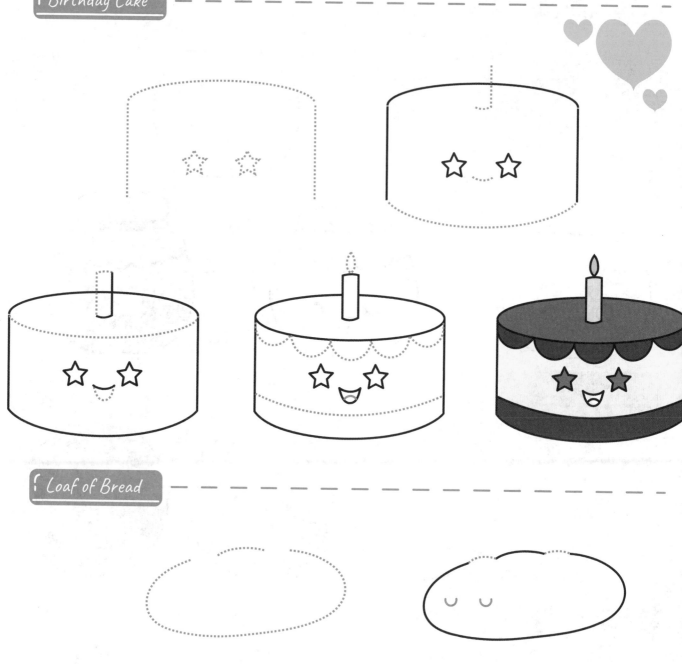

Loaf of Bread

   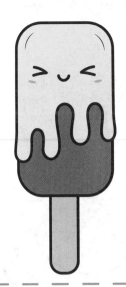

 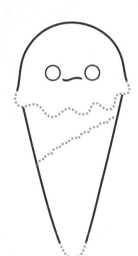  

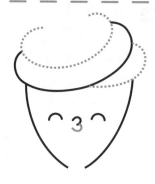

Strawberry Icecream

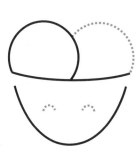

Icecream Sundae

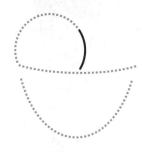

Slice of Cake

Milkshake

Strawberry Cupcake

Lollipop

Hard Candy

Macaroon

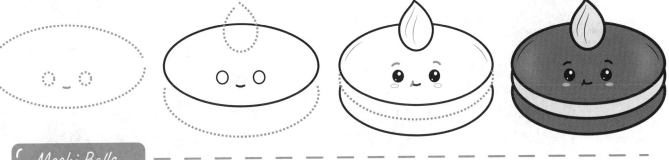

Mochi Balls

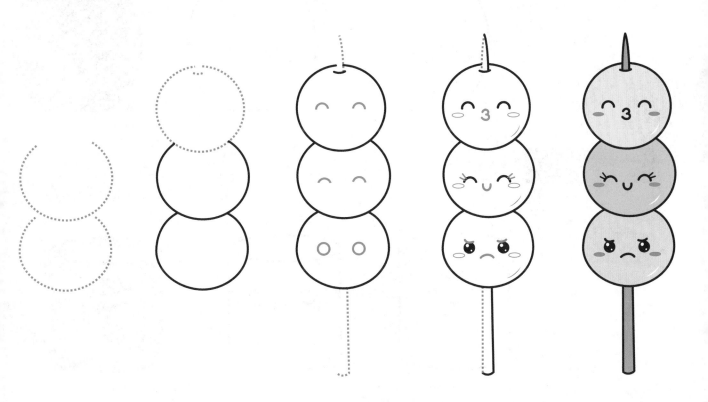

Milk

Chocolate Syrup

Hot Chocolate

DOMESTIC MAMMALS

Beagle

Chihuahua

Corgi

Pug

German Shepherd

Bassett Hound

Irish Setter

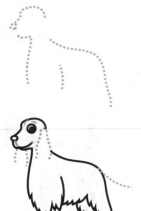  

Husky

Bernese Mountain Dog

Whippet

Great Dane

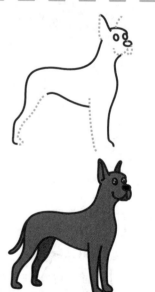

Golden Retriever

Boxer

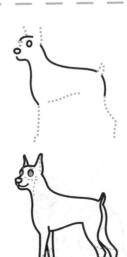

Dobermann

Pomeranian

Bulldog

French Bulldog

Pitbull

Pug Puppy

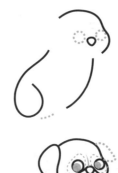

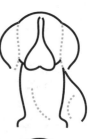

Beagle Puppy

German Shepherd Puppy

Corgi Puppy

Golden Retriever Puppy

Chihuahua Puppy

American Shorthair Cat

Russian Blue Cat

Longhair Cat

Munchkin Cat

Bengal Cat

Maine Coon Cat

Sphynx Hairless Cat

Ragdoll Kitten

American Shorthair Kitten

Munchkin Kitten

Sphynx Hairless Kitten

Norwegian Fjord Horse

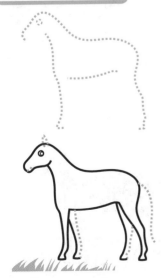

Akhal-Teke Horse

Mustang

Friesian Horse

Clydesdale Horse

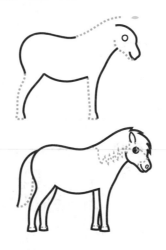

f Dales Pony

f American Miniature Pony

Sheep

Domestic Goat

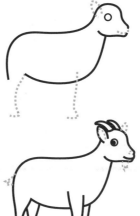

Donkey

Ox

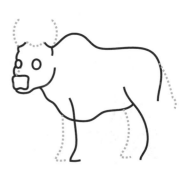

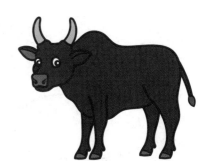

Water Buffalo

Cow

Pig

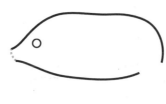

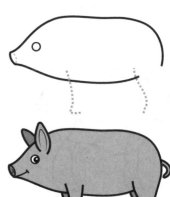

Alpaca

Rabbit

Hamster

Chinchilla

Gerbil

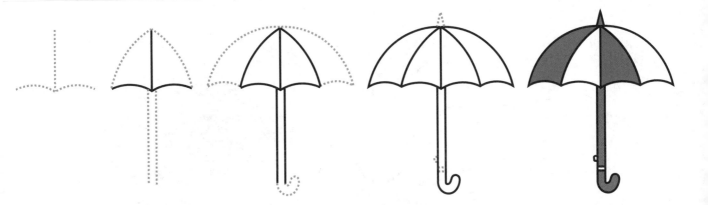

NATURE & OUTDOORS

Umbrella

Seashell

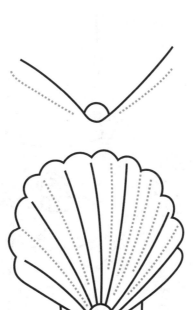

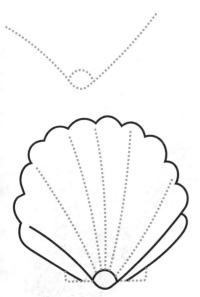

Rain Cloud

Watering Can

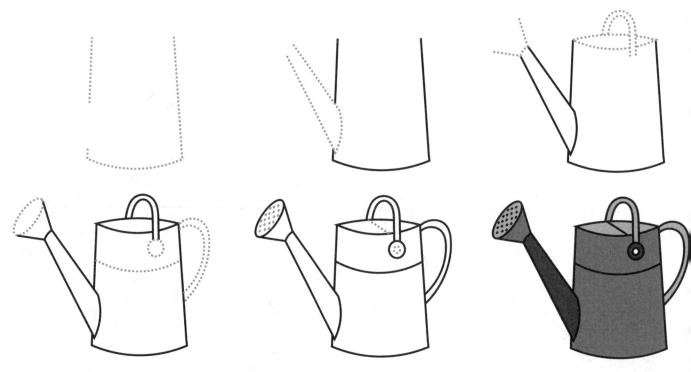

Waterfall

Pine Tree

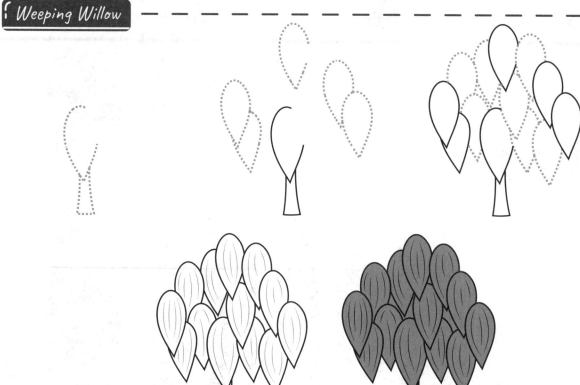

Oak Tree

Acacia Tree

ʃ Potted Cactus -

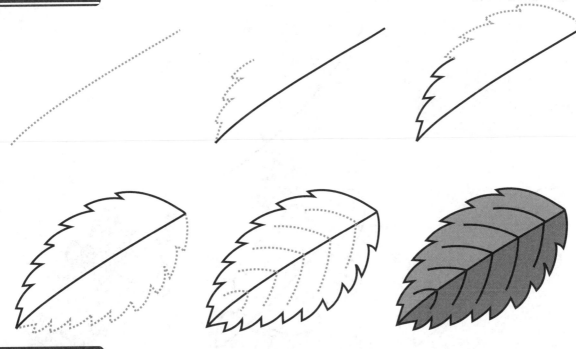

Maple Leaf

Bug Net

Birdhouse

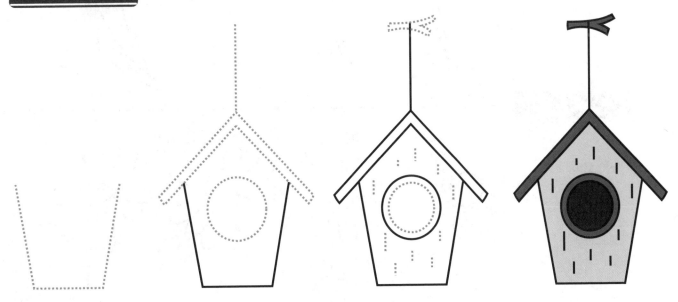

Rose

Tulip

Daisy

Lily

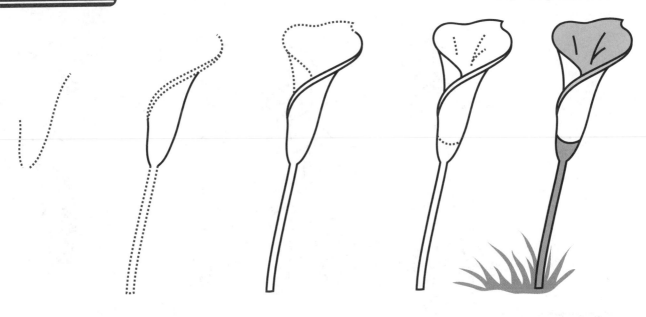

Chrysanthemum

Tulip

Toadstool

Pansy

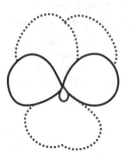

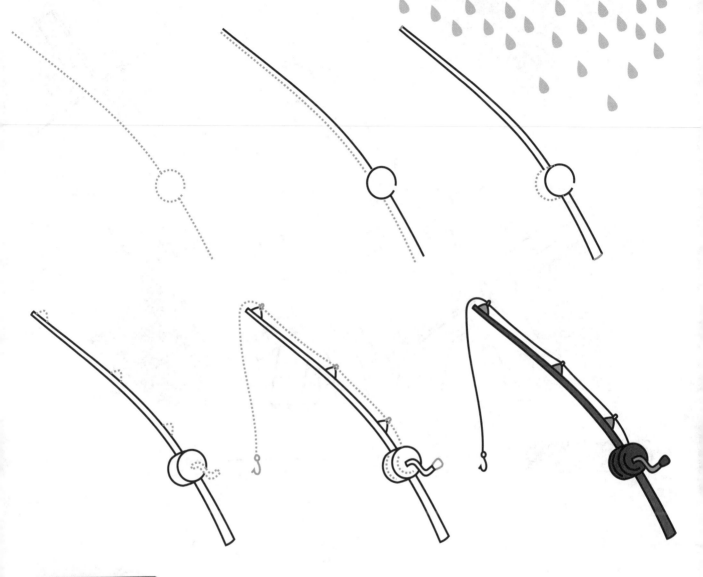

f Feather

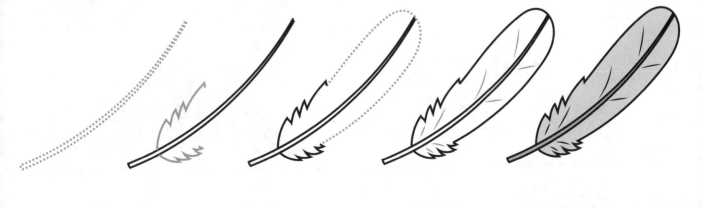

Windmill

Mountains

Blue Jay

Budgie

Cardinal

Hummingbird

Crane

Common Kestrel

Chicken

Golden Eagle

Bald Eagle

Long-Crested Eagle

Steller's Sea Eagle

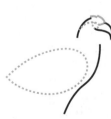

White Hawk

Gyrfalcon

Eurasian Sparrowhawk

Flamingo

Kookaburra

Great Hornbill

Emu

Quail

Ostrich

Lark

Snowy Owl

Screech Owl

Great Horned Owl

Scarlet Macaw

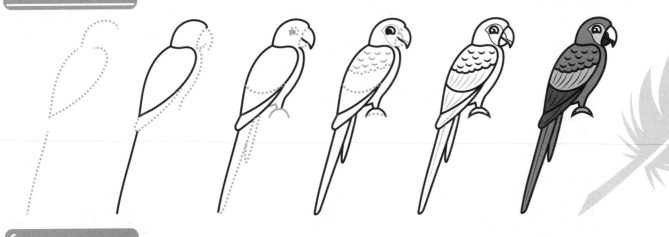

Rose-Breasted Cockatoo

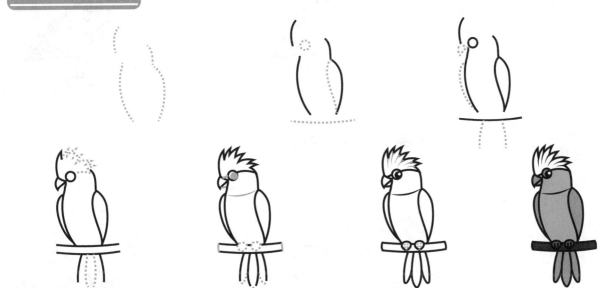

Blue Crown Conure

Rooster

Roadrunner

Raven

Swan

 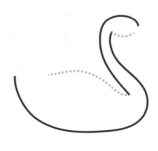 

Peacock

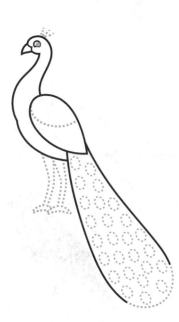  

Turkey

INSECTS

Ant

Ant Queen

Firefly

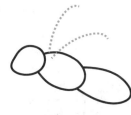

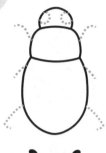

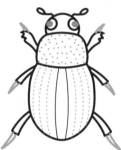

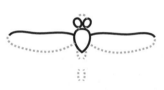
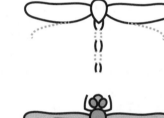

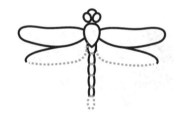

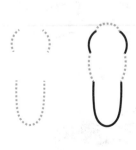
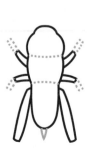
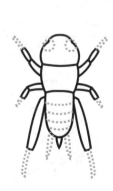
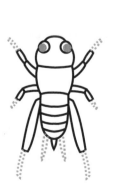

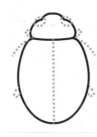

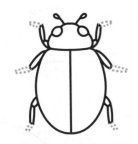

House Fly

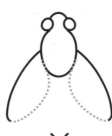

Indian Stick Insect

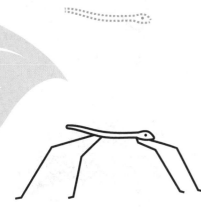
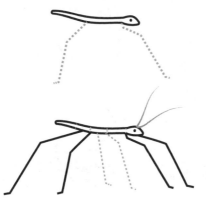
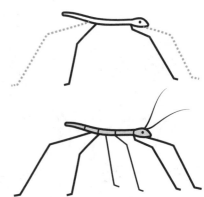

Monarch Butterfly

Rhinoceros Beetle

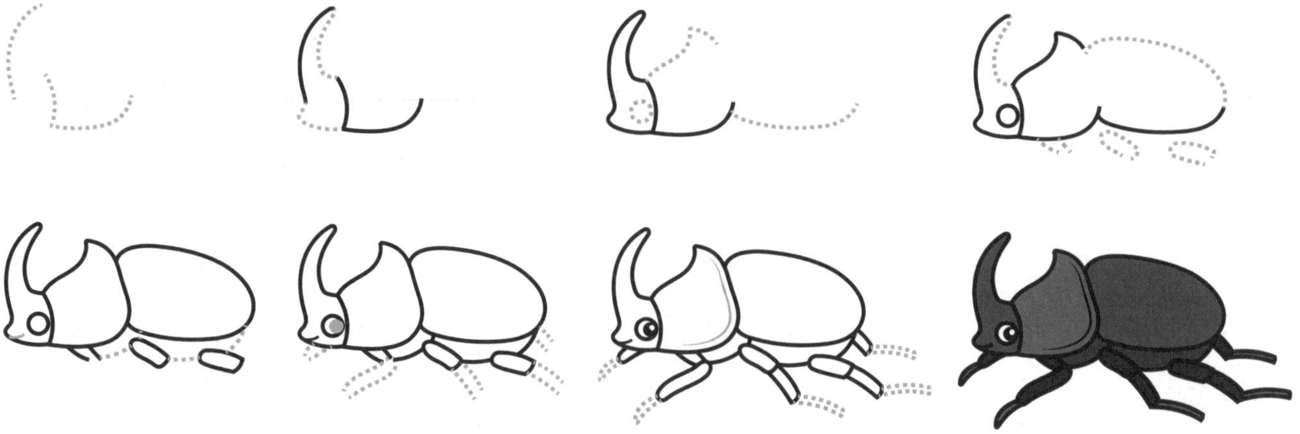

Papilio Ulysses Caterpillar

Papilio Ulysses Butterfly

Stag Beetle

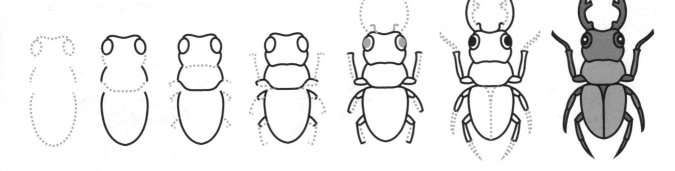

Hornet

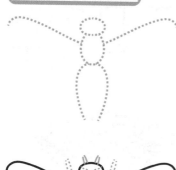  

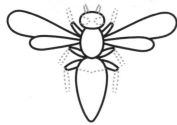  

Bumble Bee

Wasp

  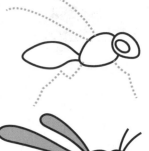

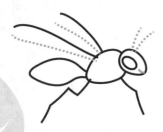  

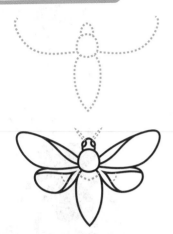
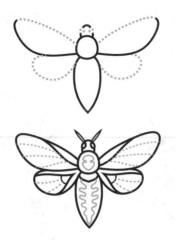
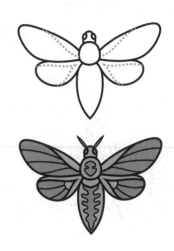

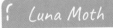

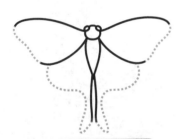

Luna Moth

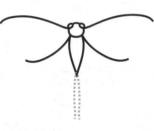

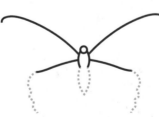

Swallowtail Butterfly

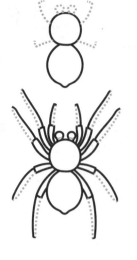
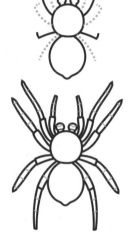

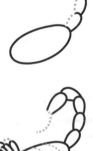
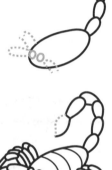
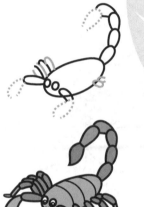

Scorpion

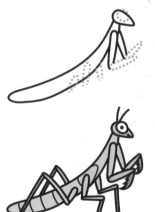

Praying Mantis

WATER ANIMALS

Betta

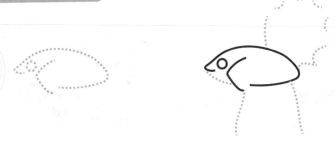

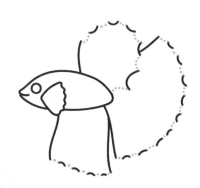

Oscar

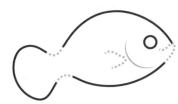

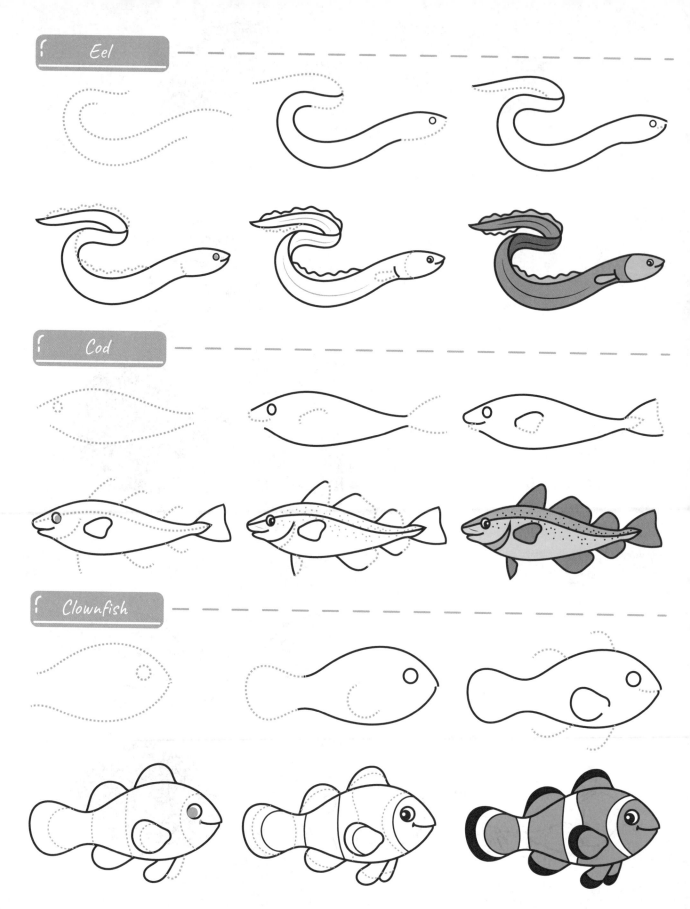

Eel

Cod

Clownfish

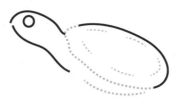
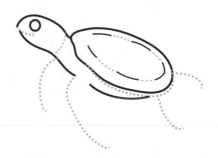

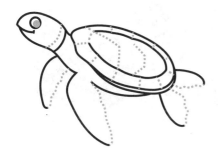

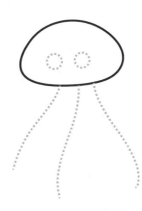

Jellyfish

Crab

Narwhal

Tiger Shark

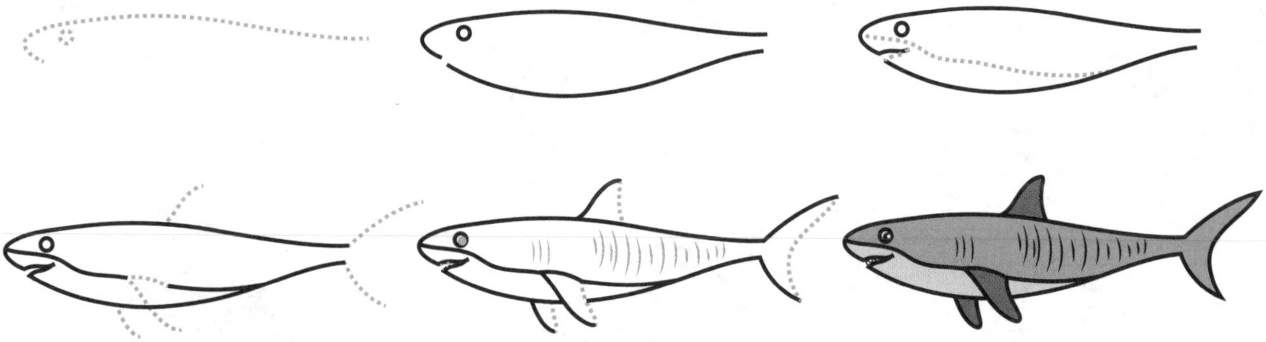

Pygmy Shark

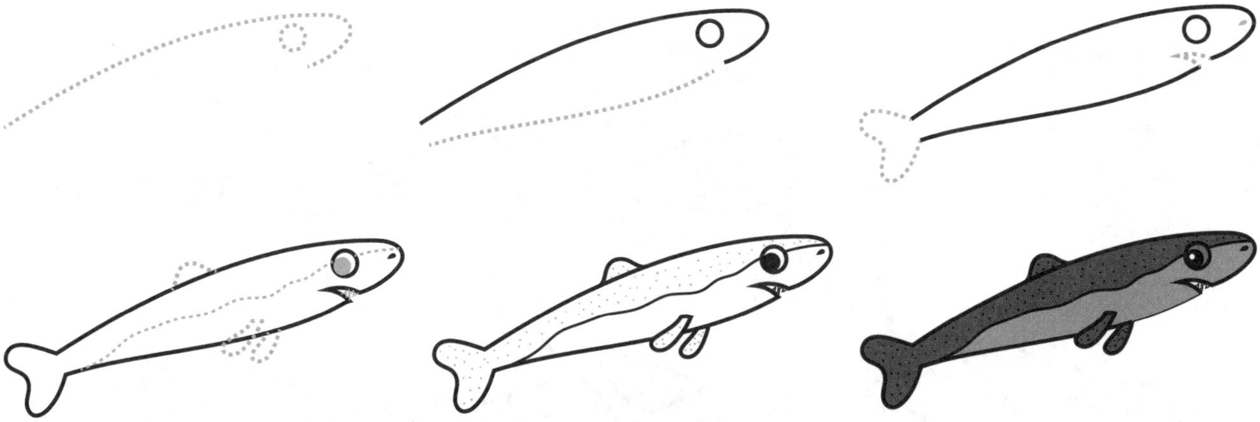

Great White Shark

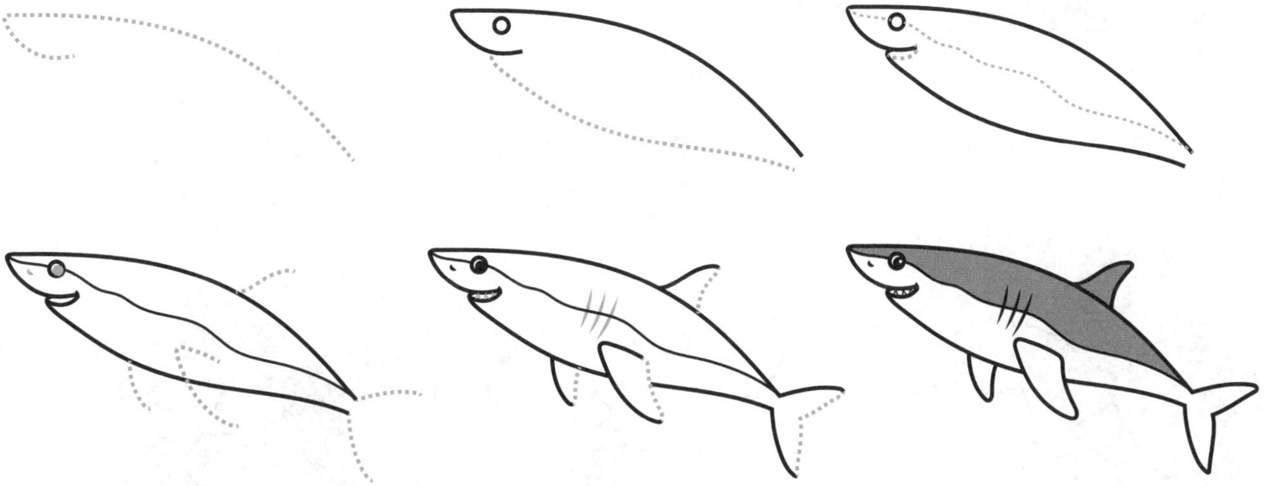

Discus

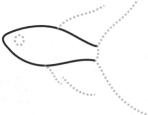

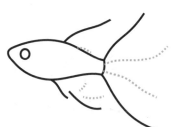

Guppy

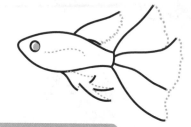

Goldfish

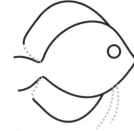

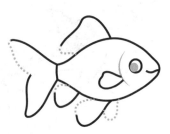

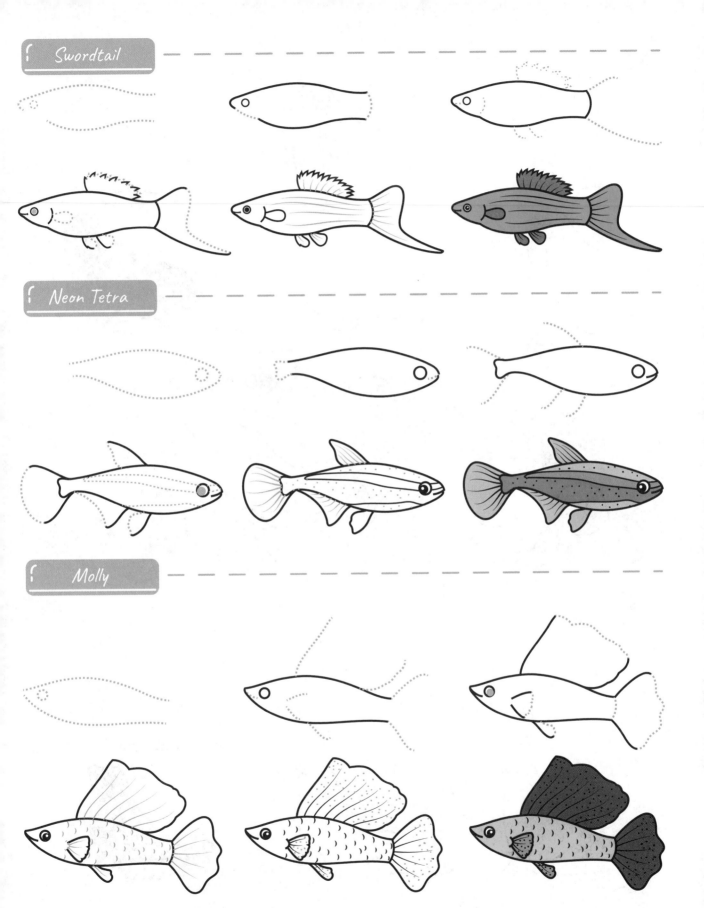

Swordtail

Neon Tetra

Molly

Walrus

Spotted Sea

Steller Sea Lion

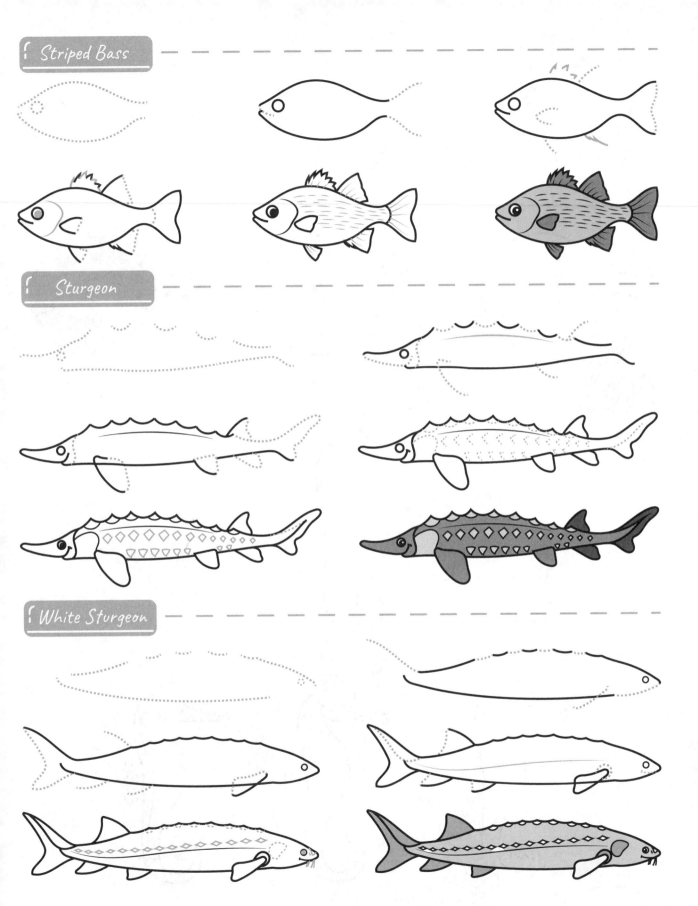

Sturgeon

White Sturgeon

Pufferfish

Seahorse

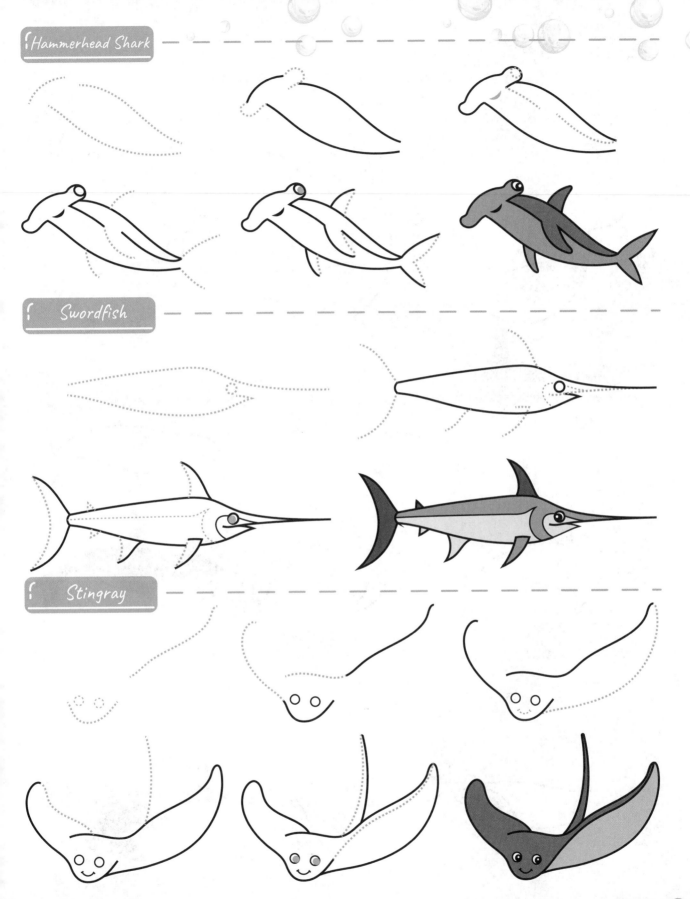

Hammerhead Shark

Swordfish

Stingray

Killer Whale

Blue Whale

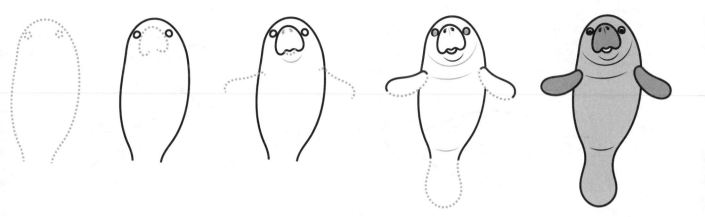

Dolphin

Sockeye Salmon

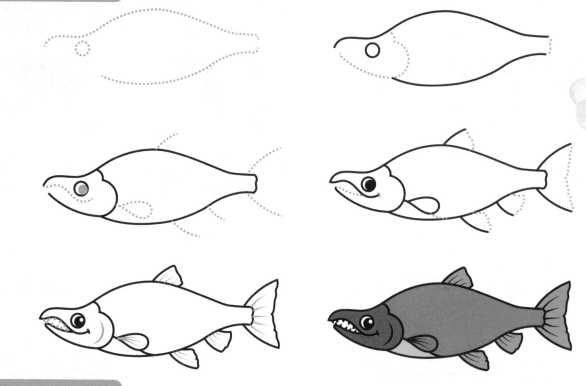

Trout

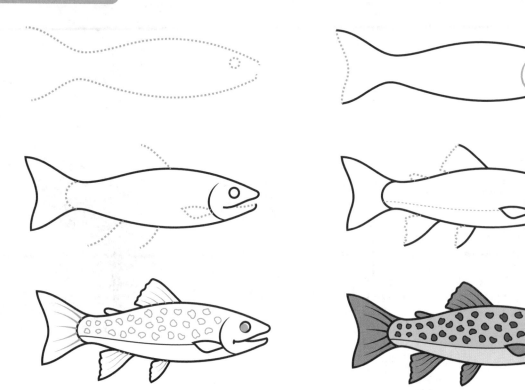

Lobster

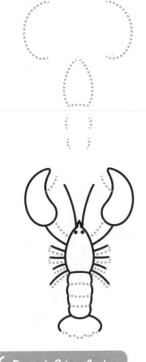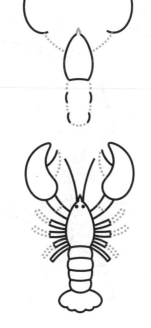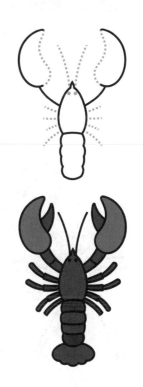

Royal Starfish

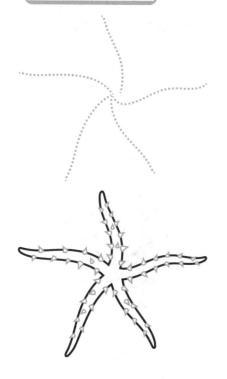
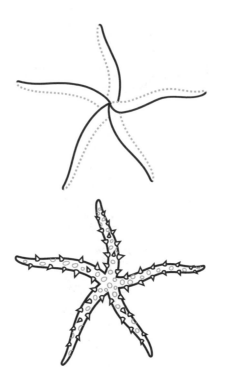
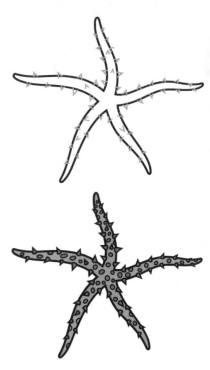

Australian Southern
Sand Star

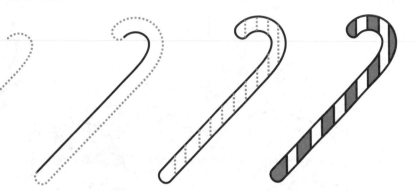
Candy Cane

Gingerbread Man

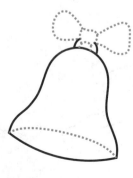

Holiday Bell

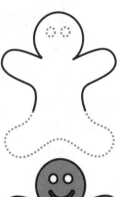

Ornament

Christmas Tree

Christmas Elf

Peace Dove

Dreidel

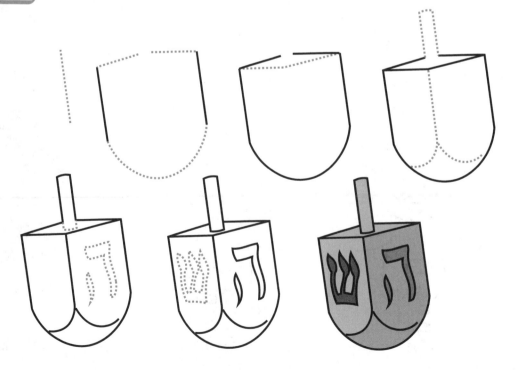

Menorah

Sled

Snowman

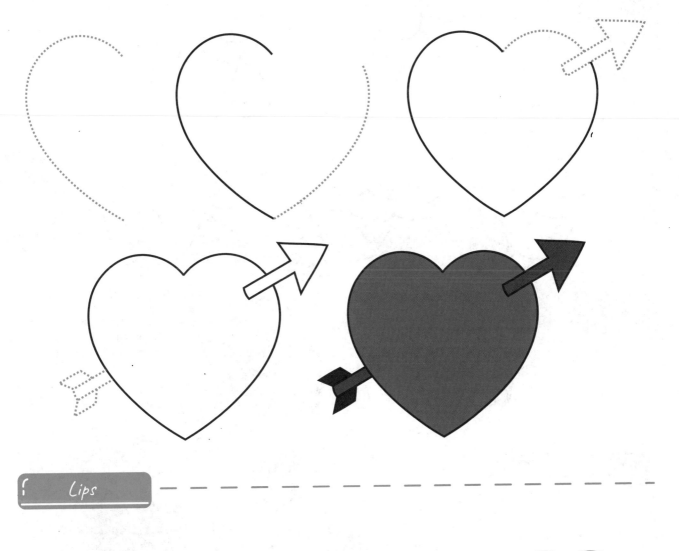

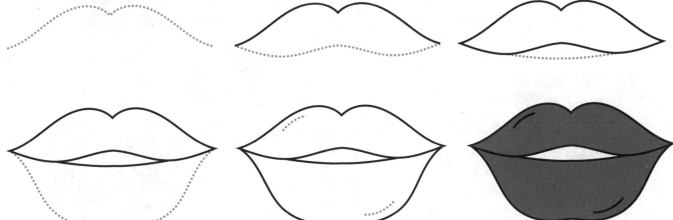

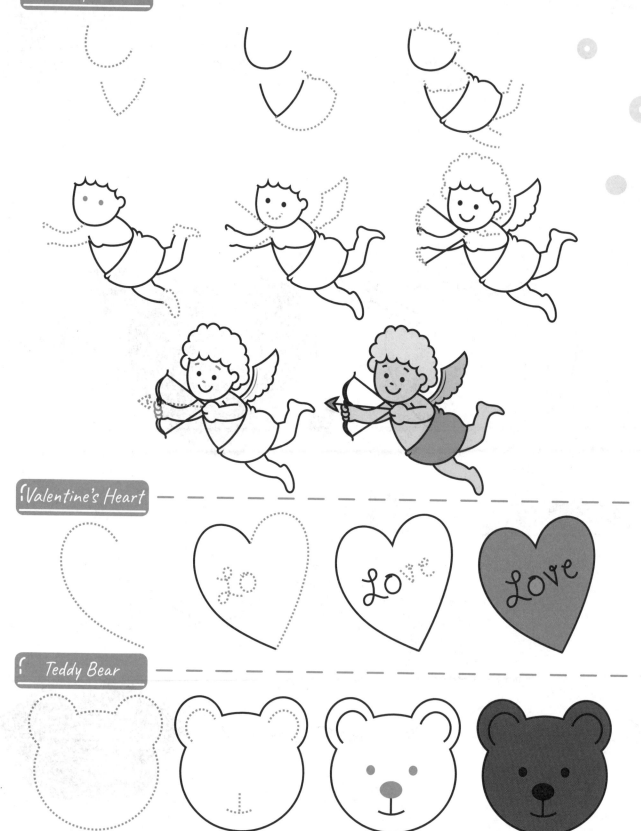

Cupid

Valentine's Heart

Love

Teddy Bear

Clover

Easter Bunny

Easter Egg

Balloons

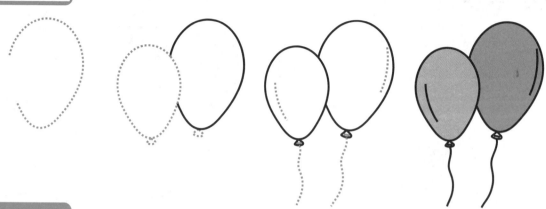

Two-tiered Cake

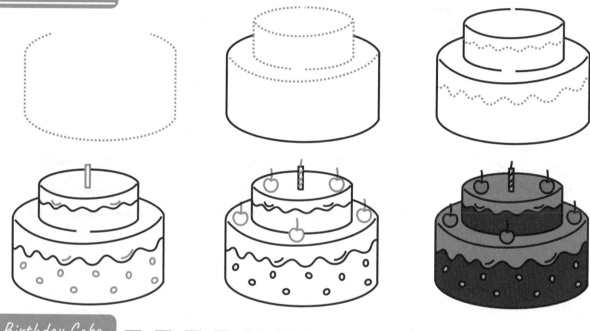

Birthday Cake

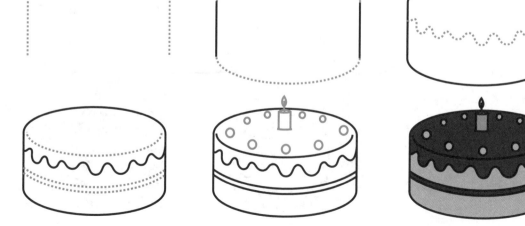

Party Hat

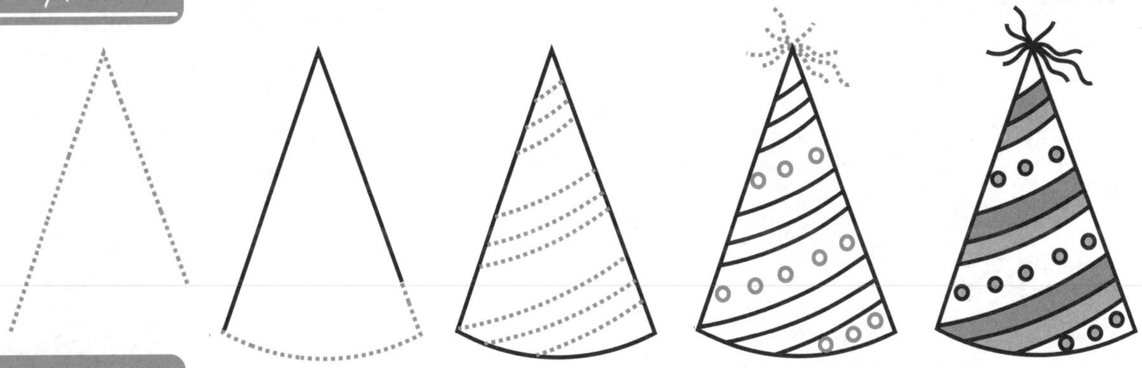

Beach Pail

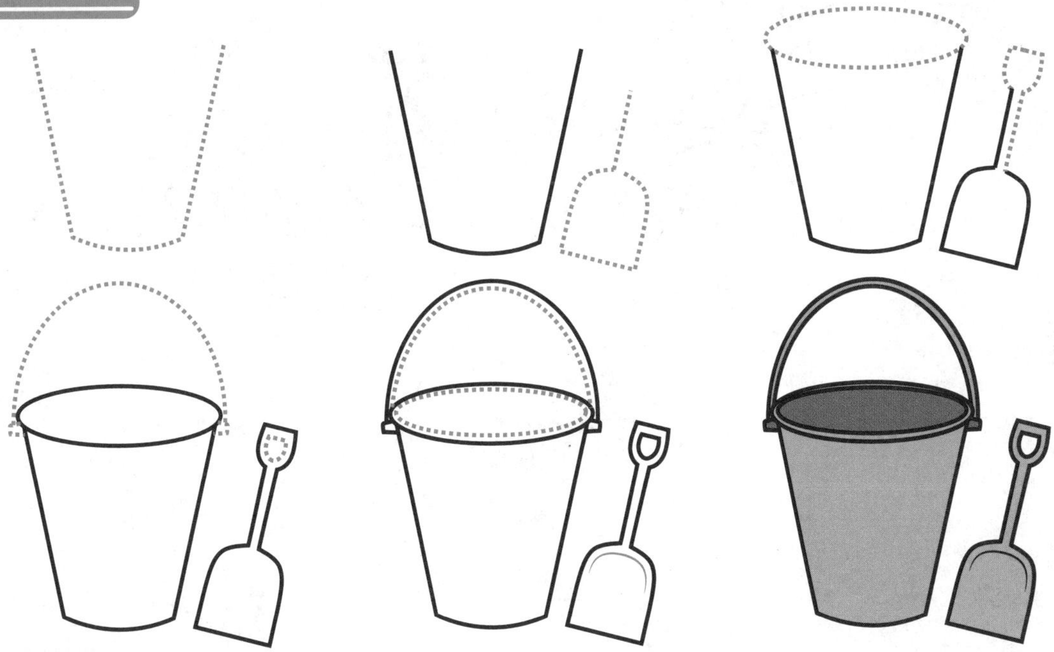

Stereo

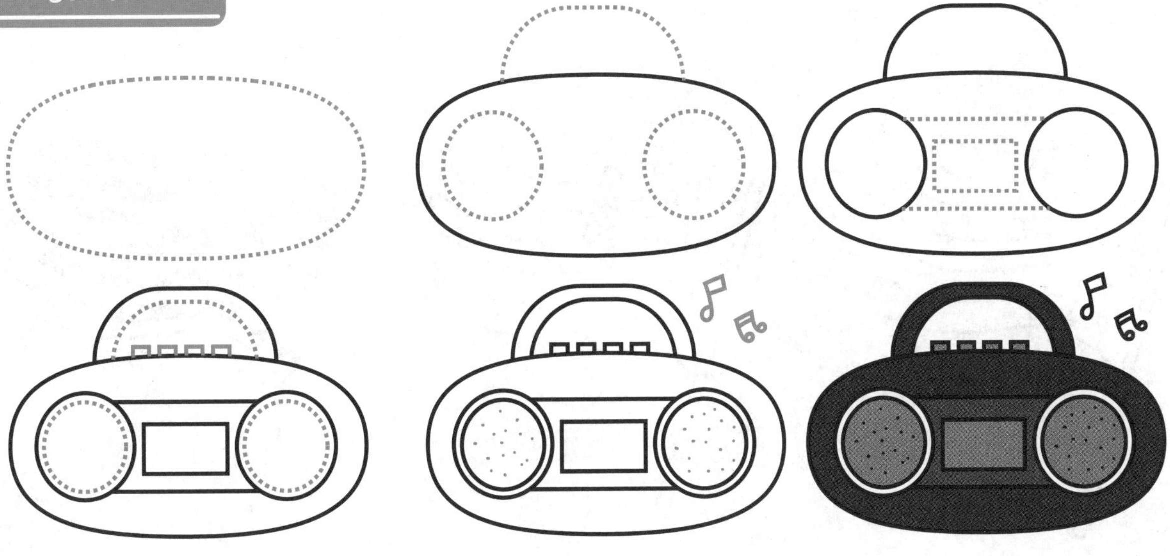

Fireworks

USA Flag

f Sleeping Bag

f Backpack

Binoculars

Flashlight

Camping Fire

Witch

Grave

Ghost

Haunted House

Jack-O-Lantern

Cornucopia

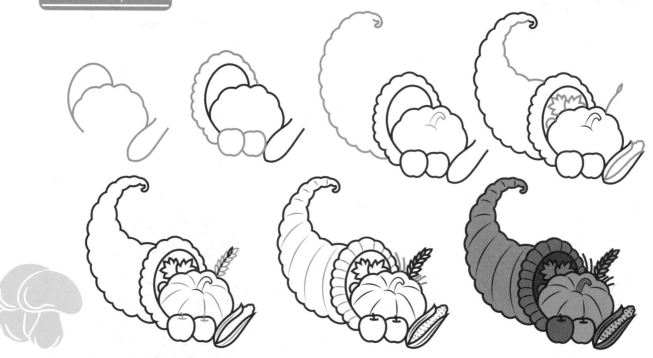

Scarecrow

WILD MAMMALS

Tiger

Snow Leopard

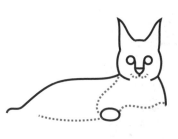

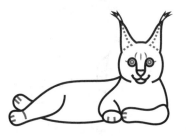

Cheetah

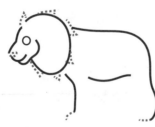

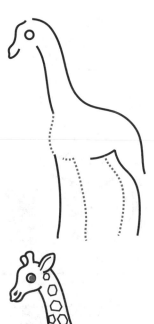
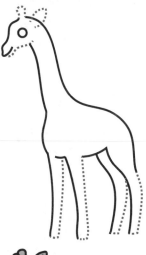

Okapi

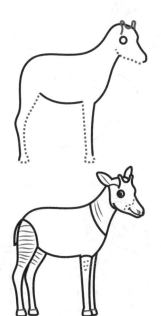

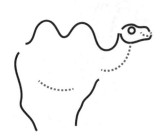

Bactrian Camel -

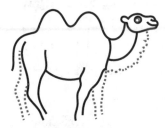

Elephant -

Gorilla

Chimpanzee

f Orangutan

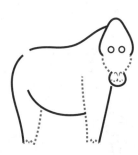
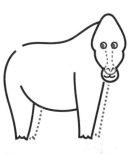

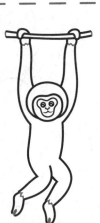

Tamarin

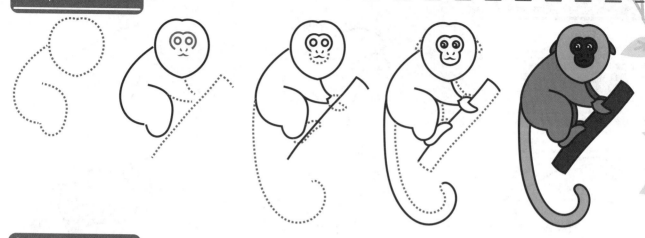

Capuchin

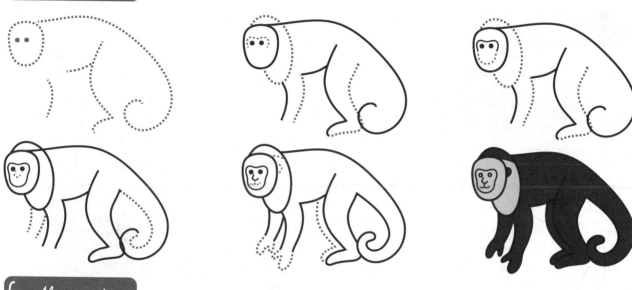

Marmoset

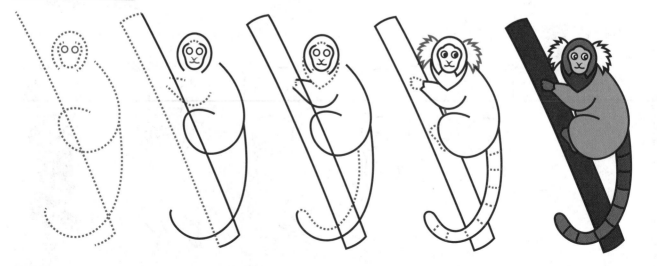

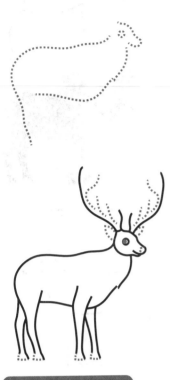

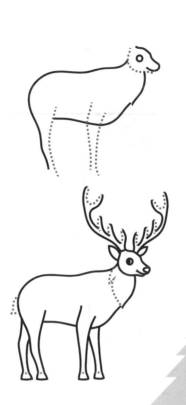

Reindeer

Dik-Dik

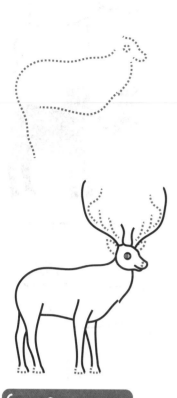
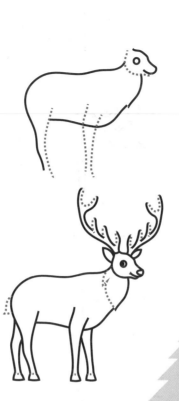

Dik-Dik

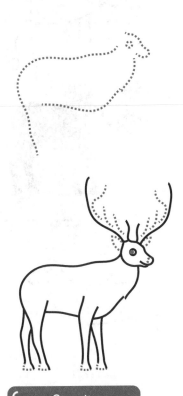
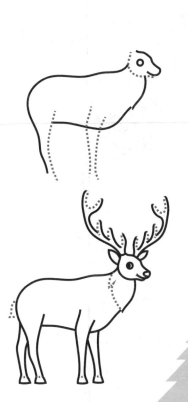

White-Tailed Deer

Mouse Deer

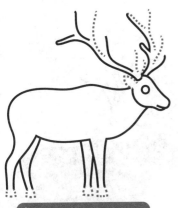

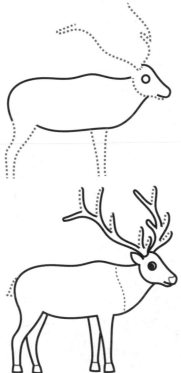

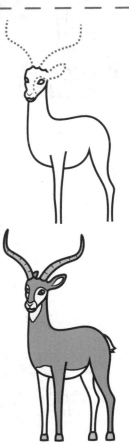

Antelope

Reindeer

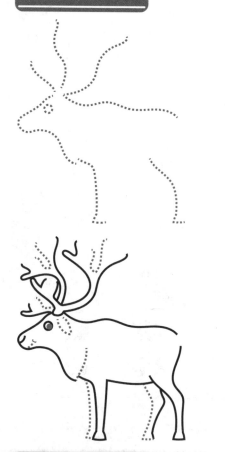

Dik-Dik

Llama

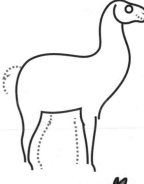

Black Bear

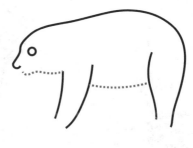

Sloth Bear

Giant Panda

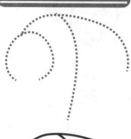
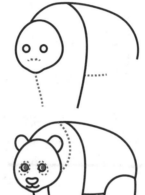

Grizzly Bear

Koala

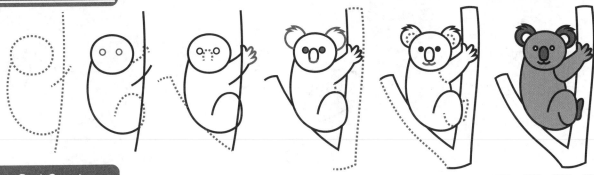

Red Panda

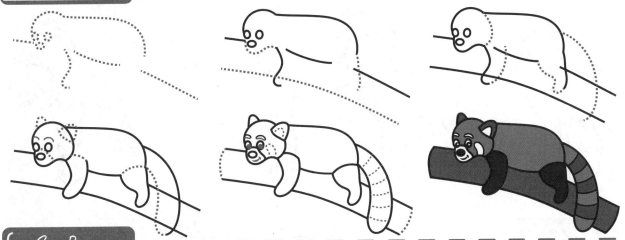

Sun Bear

Polar Bear

Argali Goat

Cape Buffalo

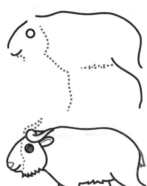

Takin

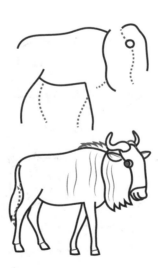

Wildebeest

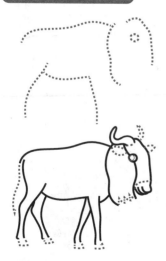

Hyena

  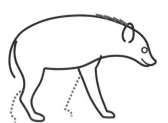

  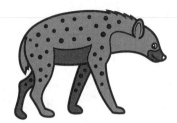

Zebra

Tapir

 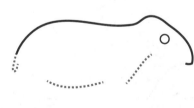 

Wild Boar

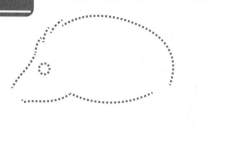 

Pangolin

 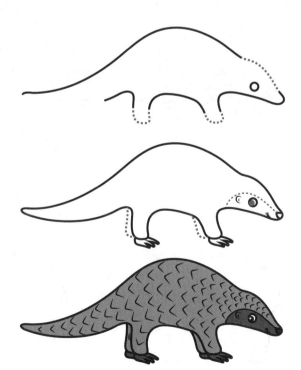

Sloth

 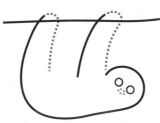 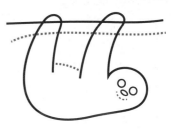

 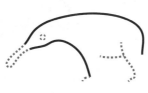 

Anteater

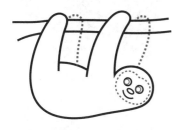  

Aardvark

Quoll

Common Brushtail Possum

Raccoon

Ring-Tailed Coati

Coyote

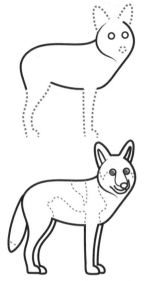

Wolf

Raccoon Dog

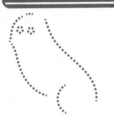

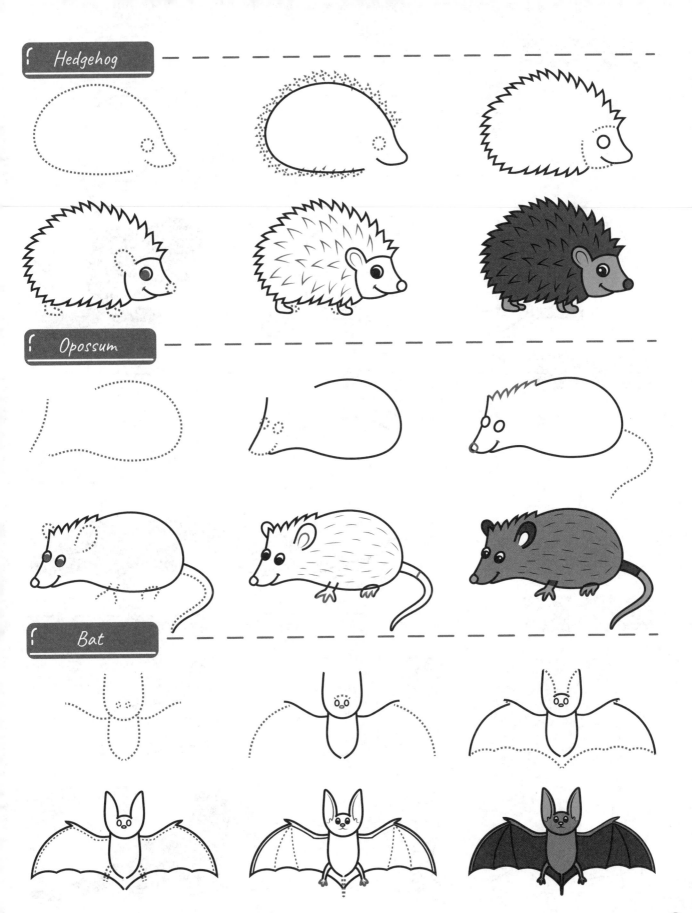

Hedgehog

Opossum

Bat

Beaver

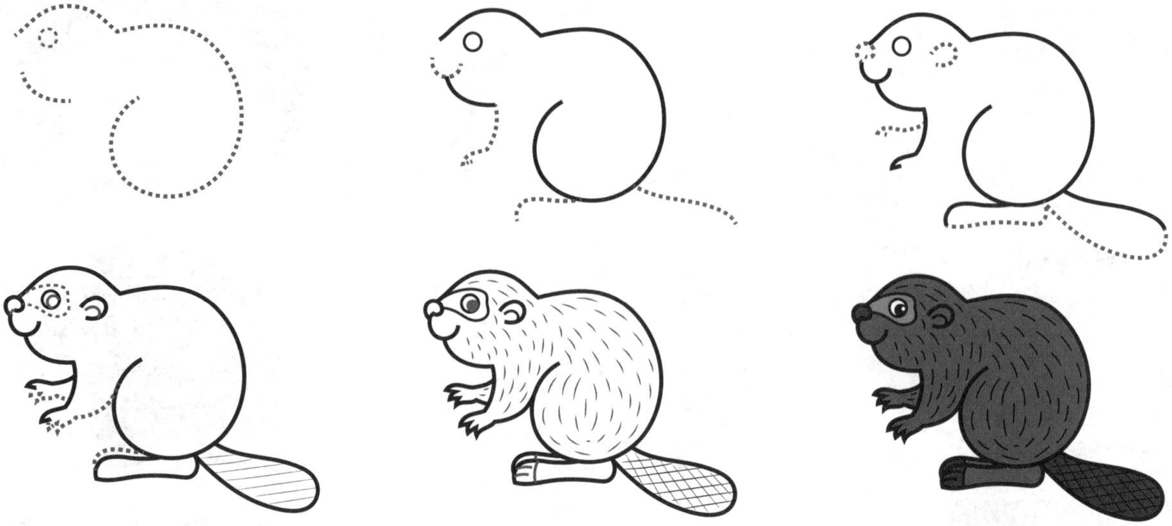

Platypus

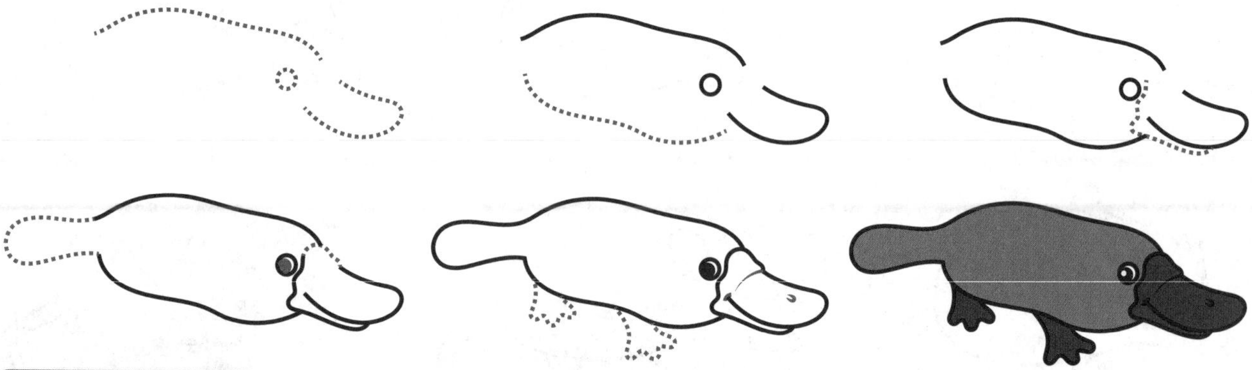

Otter

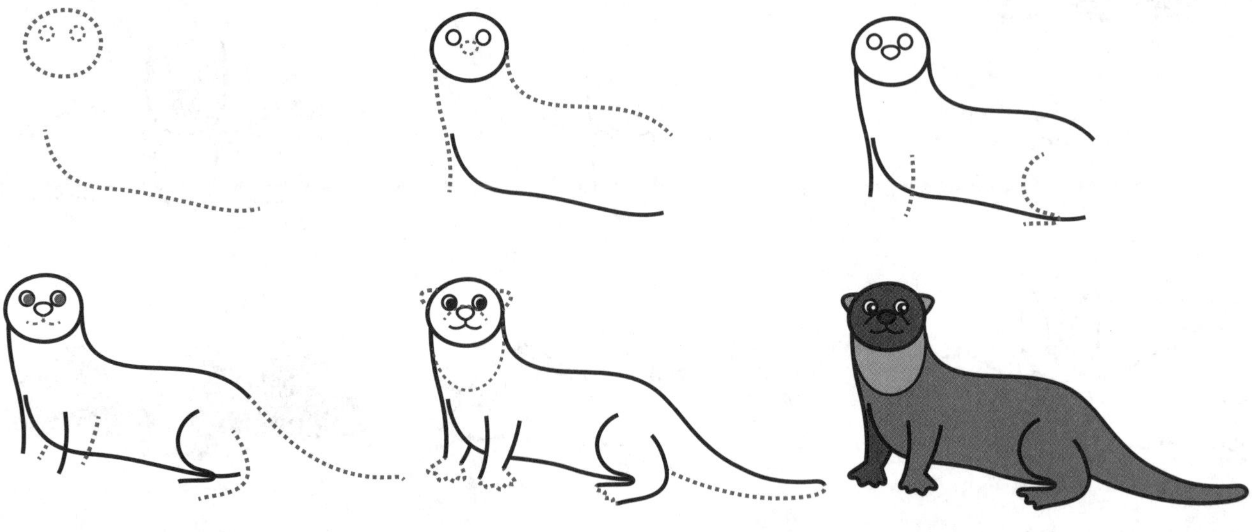

Chipmunk

Groundhog

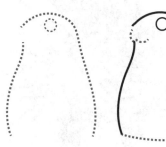

Capybara

Porcupine

Sugar Glider

 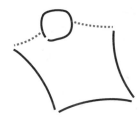 

Squirrel

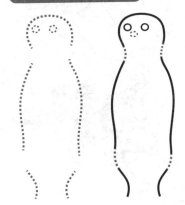  

Meerkat

 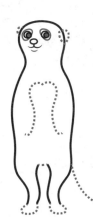  

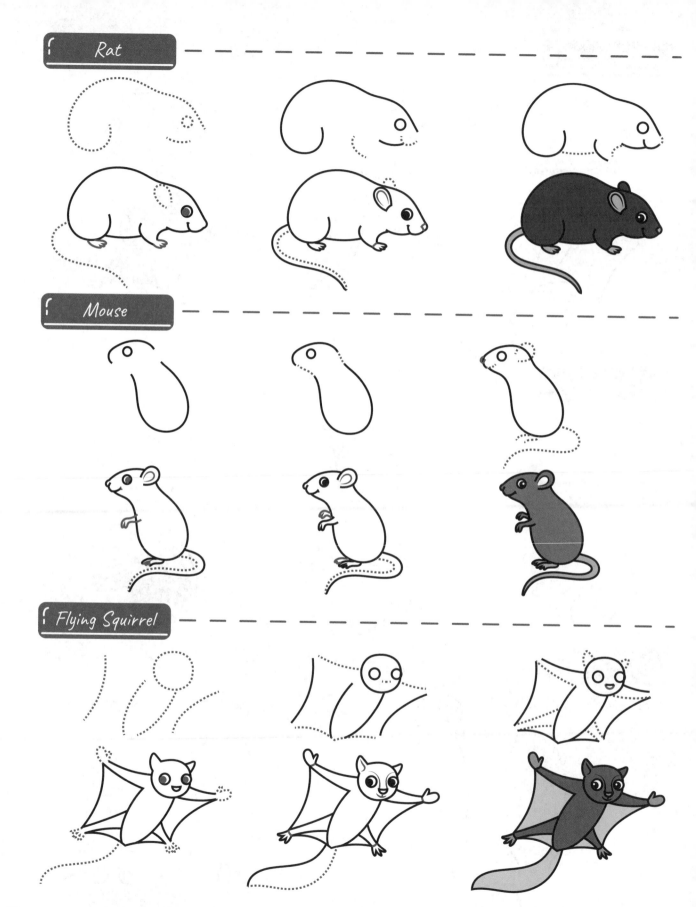

Rat

Mouse

Flying Squirrel

Iguana

Gliding Lizard

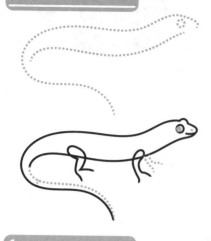

Skink

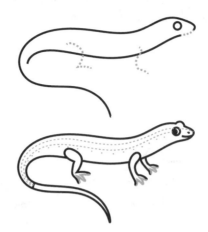

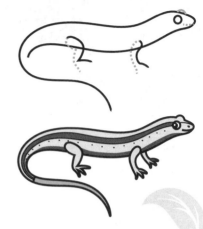

Chinese Water Dragon

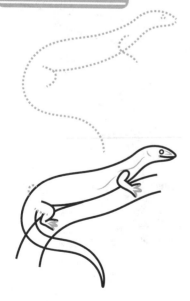

Rock Monitor

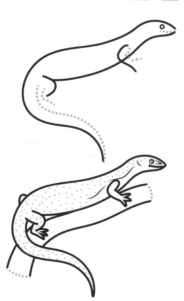

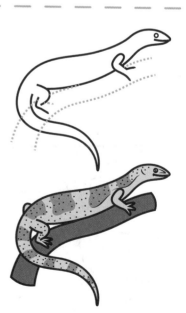

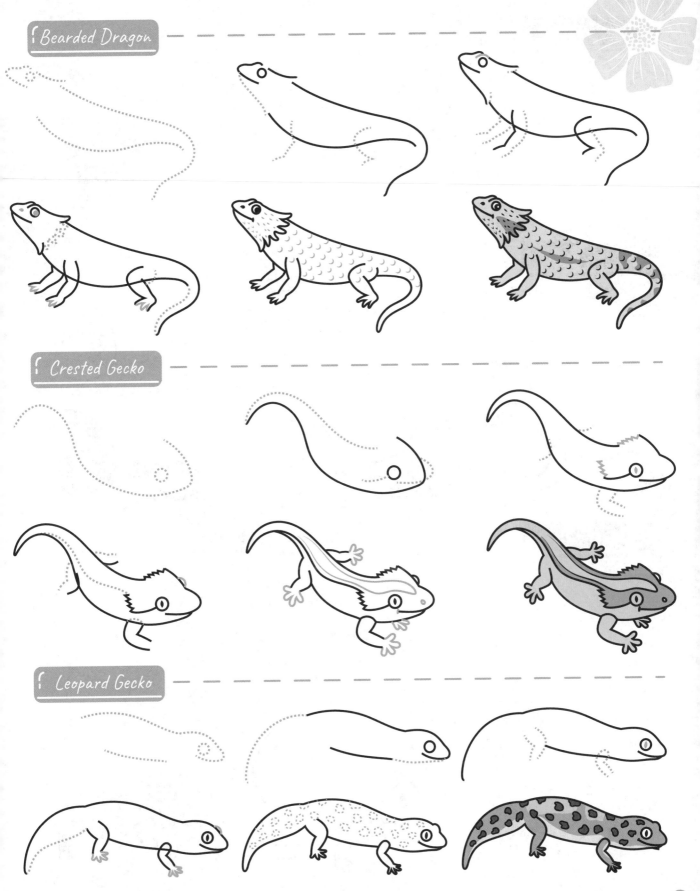

Crested Gecko

Leopard Gecko

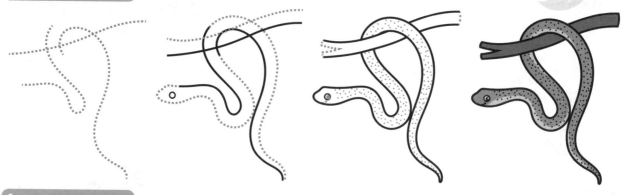

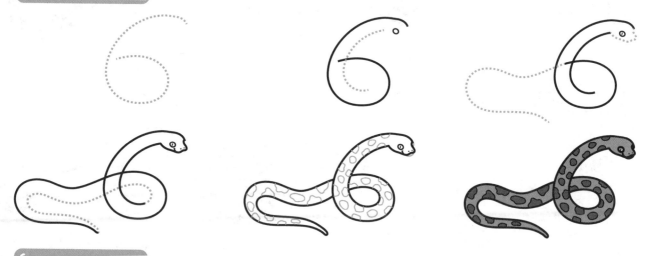

Kingsnake

Cobra

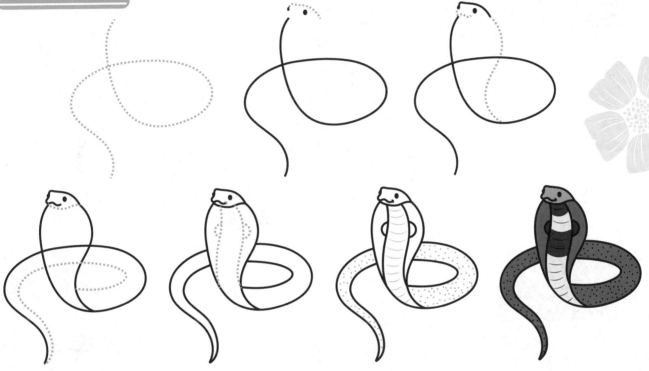

Python

Rattlesnake

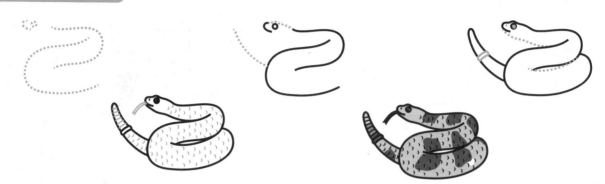

Viperidae

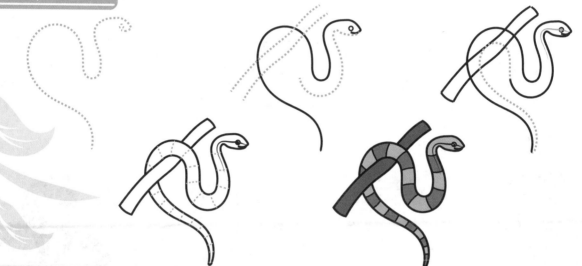

Ahaetulla

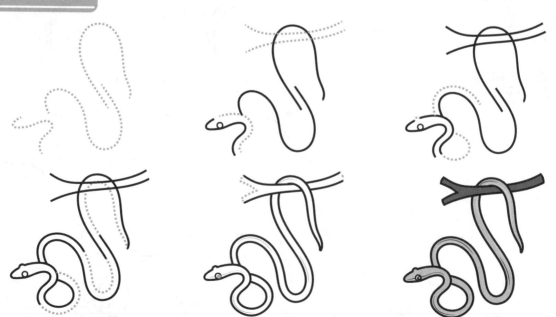

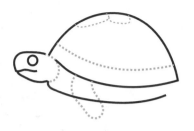

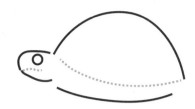

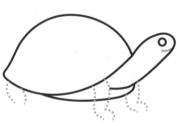

Turtle

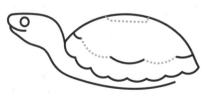

Box Turtle

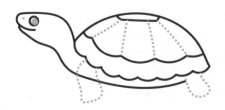

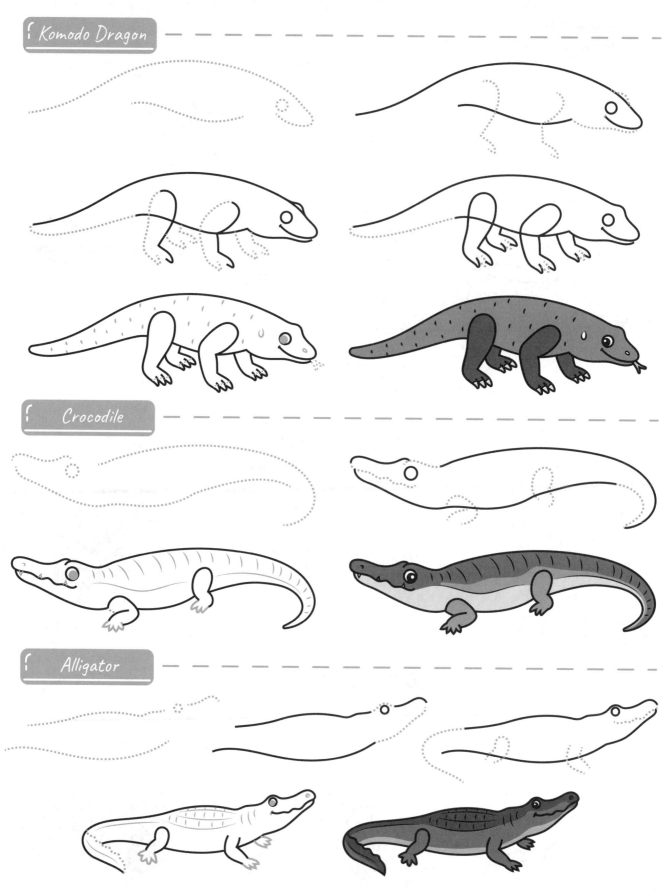

Komodo Dragon

Crocodile

Alligator

Chinese Giant Salamander

Danube Crested Newt

Common Toad

Eastern Newt

Frog Tadpole

Northern Leopard Frog

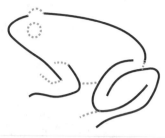

Fire Salamander

Common Reed Frog

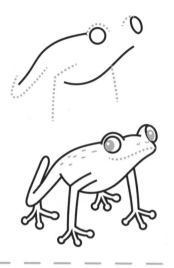

Panamanian
Golden Frog

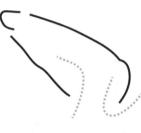
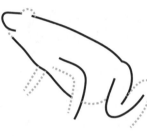

Vietnamese
Mossy Frog

DINOSAURS & FRIENDS

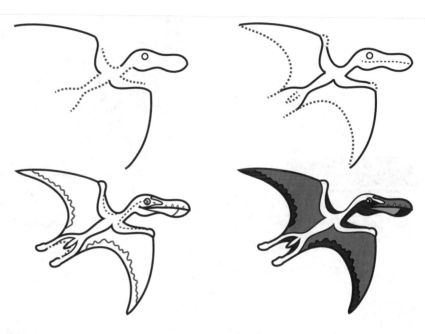

Anchiceratops

Deinonychus

Allosaurus

Baryonyx

Dilophosaurus

Albertosaurus

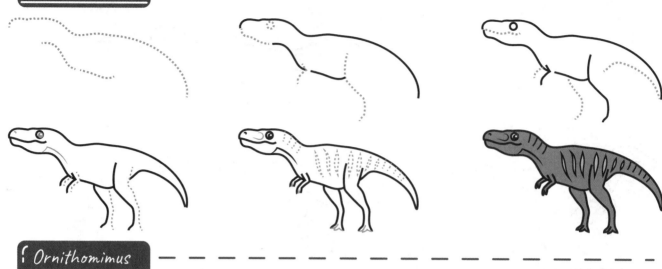

Ornithomimus

Ankylosaurus

Apatosaurus

Iguanodon

Kunbarrasaurus

Ichthyovenator

Coelophysis

Spinosaurus

Hadrosaurus

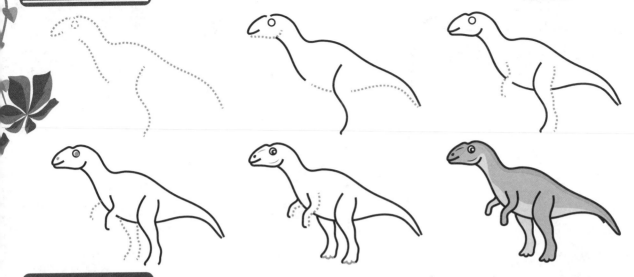

Parasaurolophus

Euoplocephalus

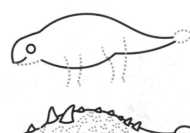

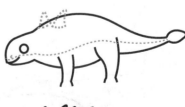

Mamenchisaurus

Velociraptor

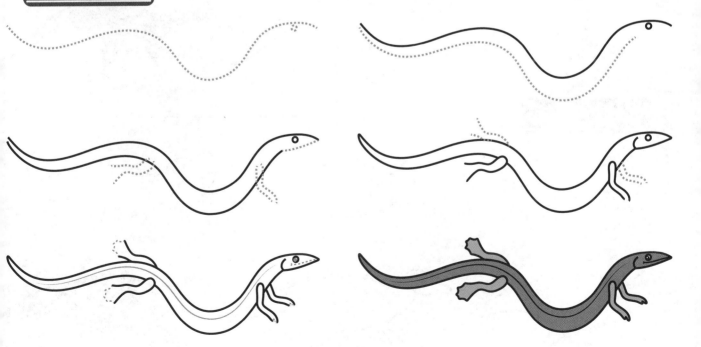

Kentrosaurus

Dilong

Edmontosaurus

Stegosaurus

Lambeosaurus

Struthiomimus

Lesothosaurus

Giganotosaurus

Tyrannosaurus Rex

Triceratops

Suchomimus

Dodo Bird

Phoenix

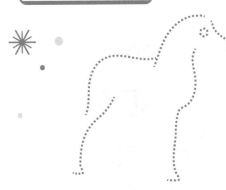

Unicorn

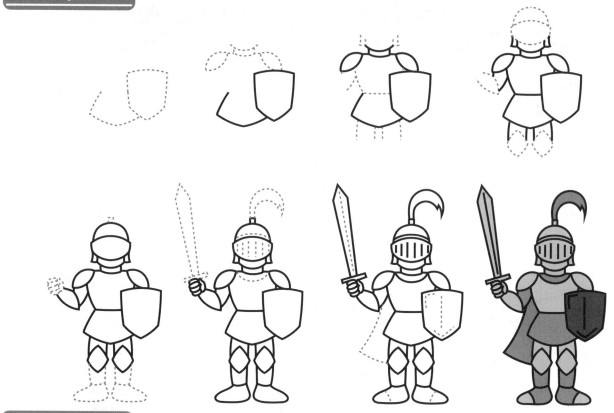

Castle

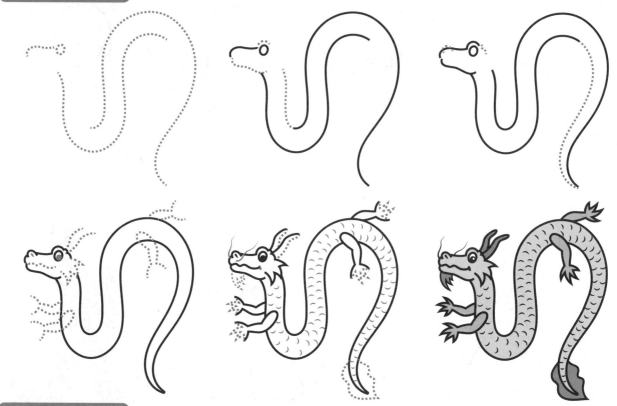

Manticore

Happy Fairy

ʄ Peryton

Hippocampus

Mermaid

Pirate

Kraken

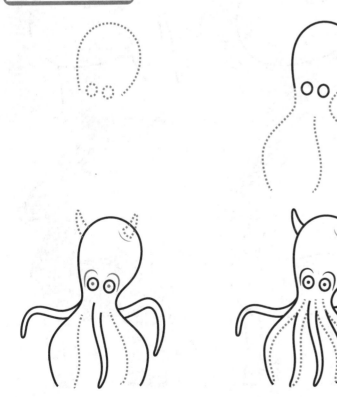

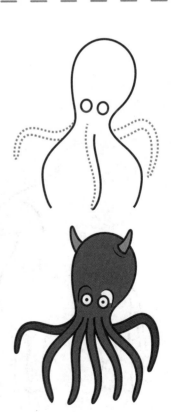

Jörmungandr

Kirin

Sphinx

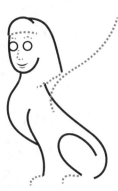

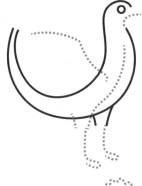

Griffin

Chimera

Chupacabra

Cerberus

Grumpy Alien

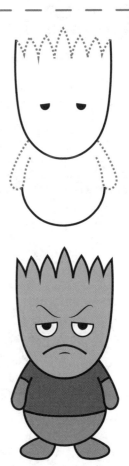

Wacky Alien

Grinning Alien

Squid Alien

U.F.O.

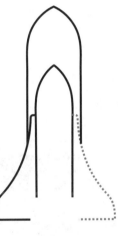

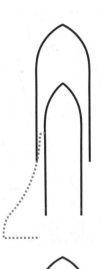

f   Space Shuttle

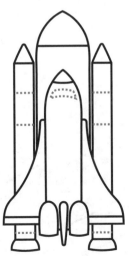

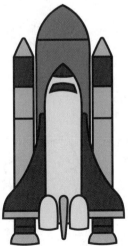

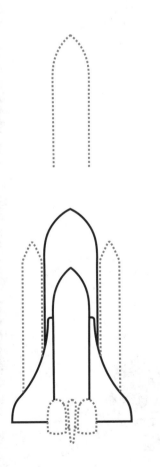

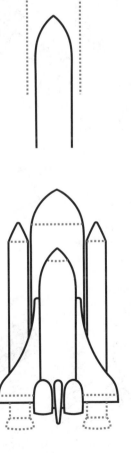

Rocket

Satellite

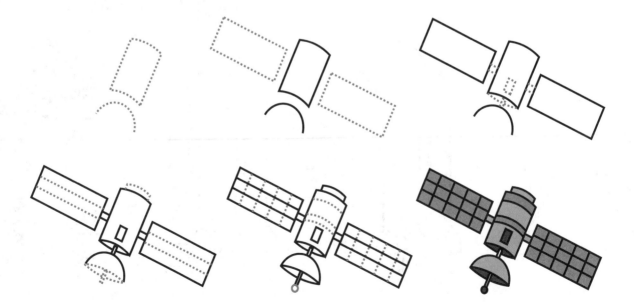

Rainbow

Planet

Moon

Astronaut

Robot

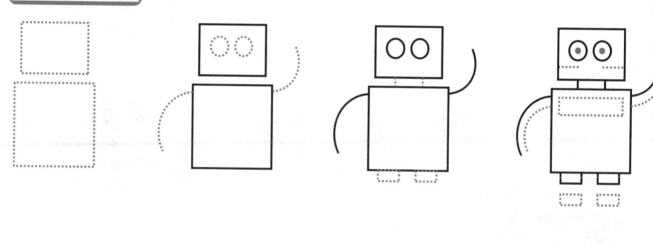

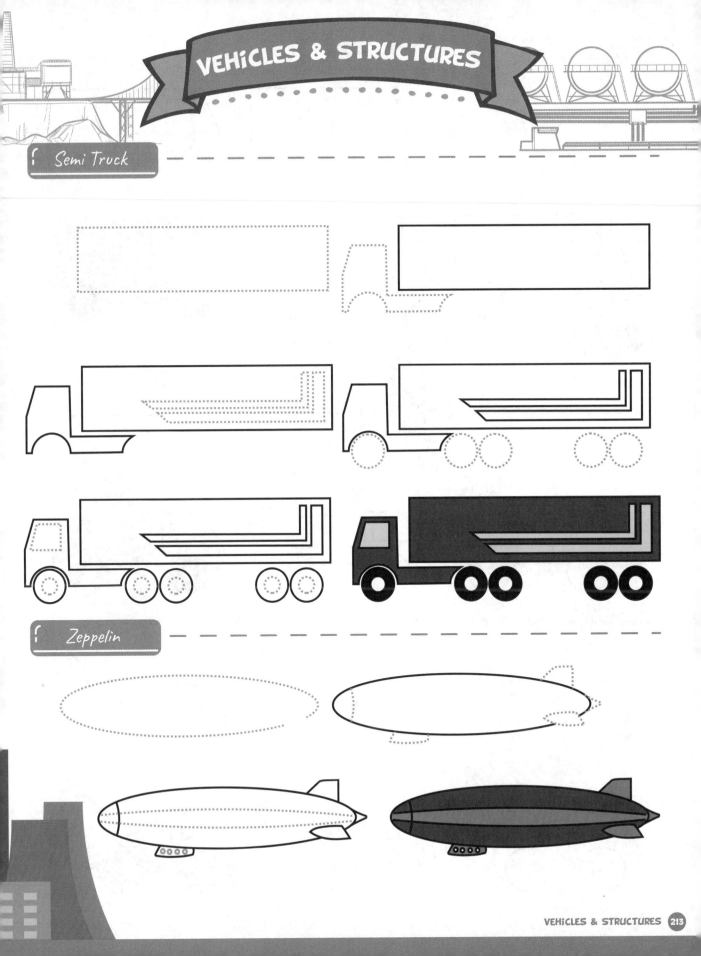

VEHiCLES & STRUCTURES

Semi Truck

Zeppelin

Bus

Dump Truck

Tow Truck

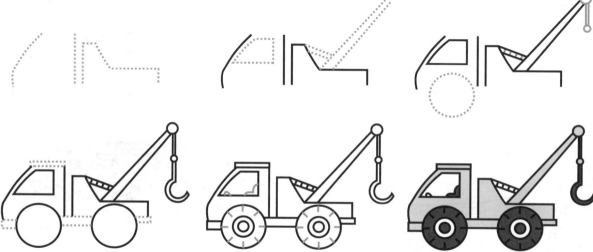

Locomotor

Train Car

Tractor

Hot Air Balloon

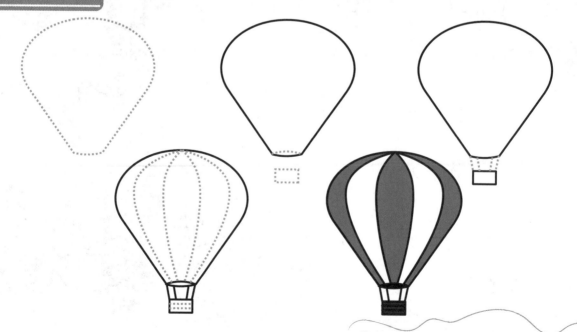

Sailboat

Bicycle

Scooter

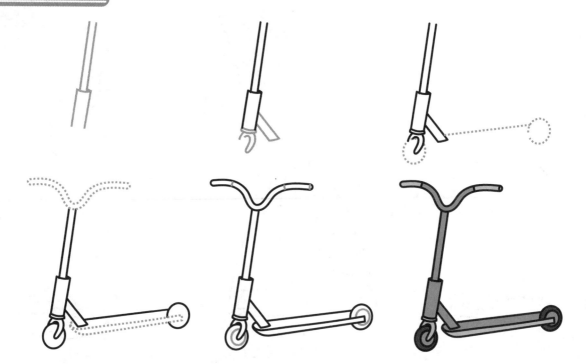

Taxi

Airplane

Schoolhouse

SCHOOL BUS

SCHOOL BUS

SCHOOL

Barn

Skyscraper

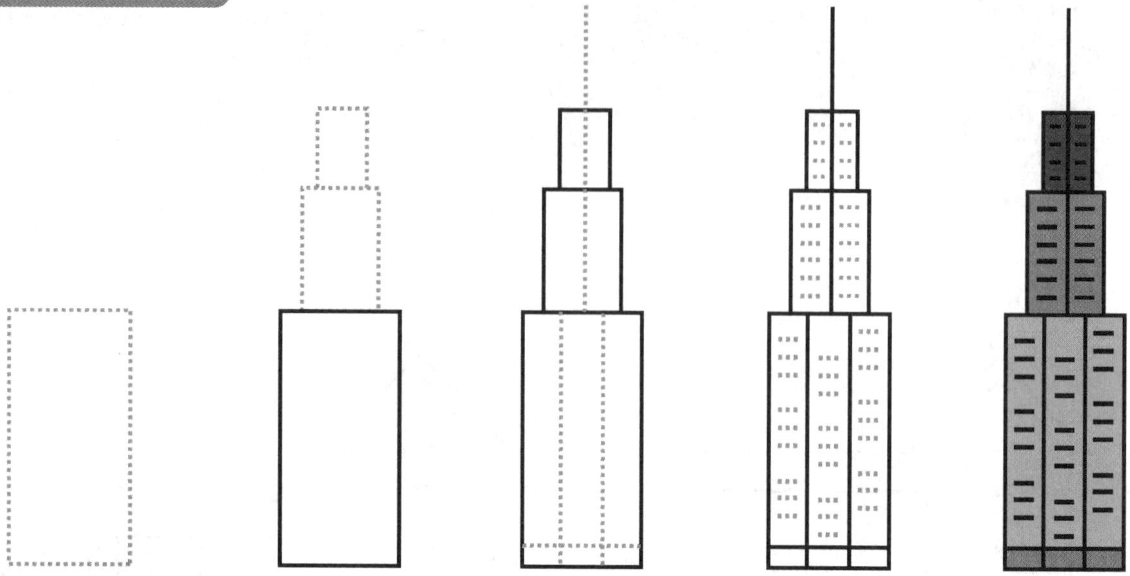

Office Building

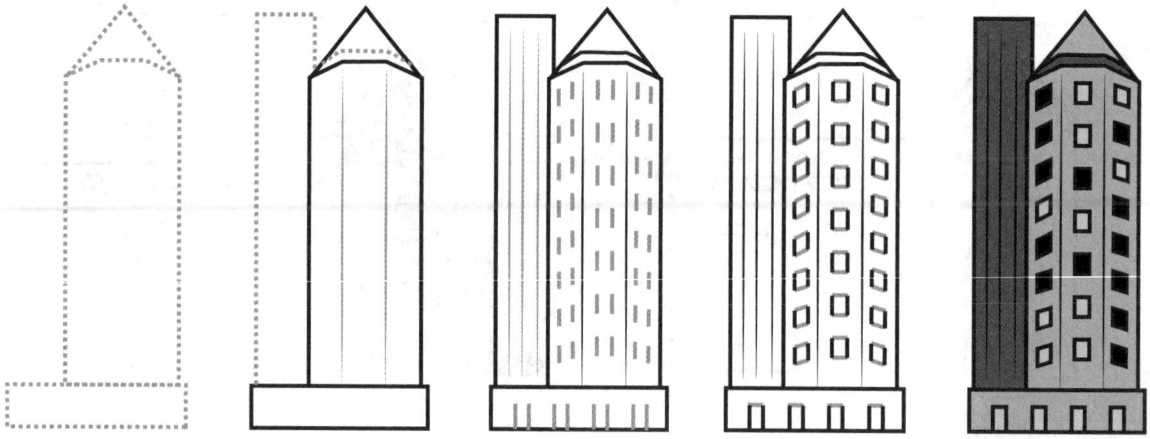

City Block

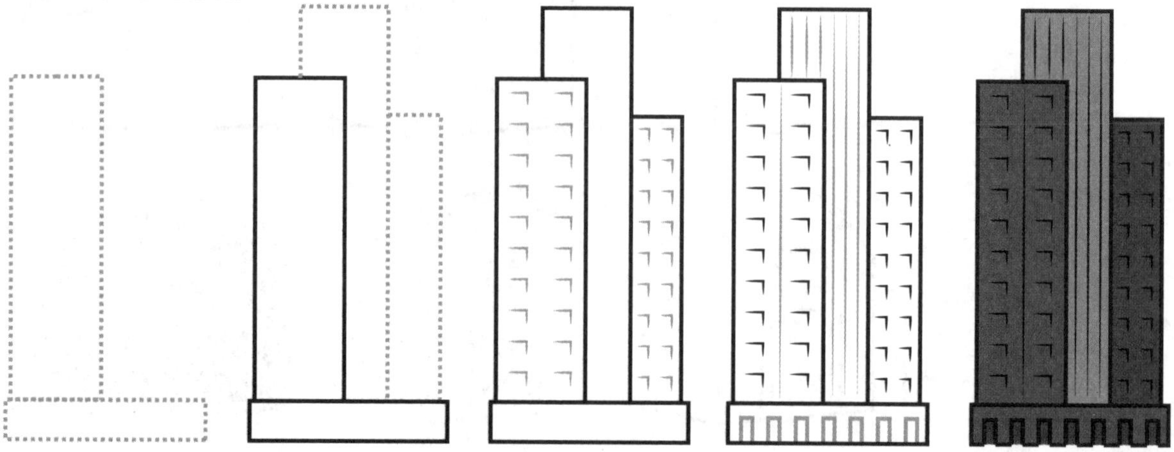

DragonFruit, an imprint of Mango Publishing, publishes high-quality children's books to inspire a love of lifelong learning in readers. DragonFruit publishes a variety of titles for kids, including children's picture books, nonfiction series, toddler activity books, pre-K activity books, science and education titles, and ABC books. Beautiful and engaging, our books celebrate diversity, spark curiosity, and capture the imaginations of parents and children alike.

Mango Publishing, established in 2014, publishes an eclectic list of books by diverse authors. We were named the Fastest Growing Independent Publisher by Publishers Weekly in 2019 and 2020. Our success is bolstered by our main goal, which is to publish high quality books that will make a positive impact in people's lives.

Our readers are our most important resource; we value your input, suggestions, and ideas. We'd love to hear from you—after all, we are publishing books for you!

Please stay in touch with us and follow us at:

Instagram: @dragonfruitkids
Facebook: Mango Publishing
Twitter: @MangoPublishing
LinkedIn: Mango Publishing
Pinterest: Mango Publishing

Sign up for our newsletter at www.mangopublishinggroup.com and receive a free book! Join us on Mango's journey to change publishing, one book at a time.

Woo! Jr. Kids' Activities is passionate about inspiring children to learn through imagination and FUN. That is why we have provided thousands of craft ideas, printables, and teacher resources to over 55 million people since 2008. We are on a mission to produce books that allow kids to build knowledge, express their talent, and grow into creative, compassionate human beings. Elementary education teachers, day care professionals, and parents have come to rely on Woo! Jr. for high quality, engaging, and innovative content that children LOVE. Our best-selling kids activity books have sold over 300,000 copies worldwide.

Tap into our free kids activity ideas at our website WooJr.com or by following us on social media:

 https://www.pinterest.com/woojrkids/
https://www.facebook.com/WooJr/
https://twitter.com/woojrkids
https://www.instagram.com/woojrkids/